# VAMPIRE AND WEREWOLF
# STORIES

*For my daughter Amy and her best friend Amelia Oliveira*

KINGFISHER
a Houghton Mifflin Company imprint
215 Park Avenue South
New York, New York 10003
www.houghtonmifflinbooks.com

First published in 1998
2 4 6 8 10 9 7 5 3
2TR/0602/THOM/---/100INDWF(W)

LIBRARY OF CONGRESS CATALOGING-IN-PUBLICATION DATA
has been applied for.

ISBN 0-7534-5152-2

Printed in India

# VAMPIRE AND WEREWOLF
## STORIES

CHOSEN BY
**ALAN DURANT**

ILLUSTRATED BY
**NICK HARDCASTLE**

KING*f*ISHER

NEW YORK

# CONTENTS

# INTRODUCTION

VAMPIRES HAVE ALWAYS given me the creeps: those piercing red eyes with their sinister, hypnotic powers, those sharp, menacing fangs and all that bloodsucking : . . . . Werewolves, on the other hand, have a pathetic quality about them that I find somehow endearing. Whereas vampires are cool and calculating in their malevolence, werewolves have the air of desperate, cursed creatures, acting from some unhappy compulsion. This may have something to do with the way the creatures were portrayed in the horror films I saw when young: Dracula was a suave, cunning, remorselessly evil villain, while the Wolf Man was a hairy, snarling, but rather brainless beast. Both creatures, though, have inspired a rich and varied literature—and indeed continue to do so. Vampire stories, in particular, appear in print with amazing regularity.

The myth of vampires is not new, of course—even the Ancient Greeks had their bloodsuckers (they were female demons called Lamiae)—but since the nineteenth century their popularity as literary subjects has grown enormously. Much of this is due to one book, Bram Stoker's *Dracula*, the most famous vampire story of all. It's a very long book and, to my mind, often tedious, but it has some exceptional, hair-raising moments, as I hope you will agree on reading the extract I have included here. But as a thrilling tale of terror, I prefer Clemence Housman's "The Werewolf," a classic of its kind, from which I've also included an extract. I encourage you to read the whole thing.

Some of these tales you may already have encountered—for example, the ironically macabre "Gabriel-Ernest" by Saki, and Arthur Conan Doyle's ingenious "The Adventure of the Sussex Vampire," which features his celebrated detective, Sherlock Holmes (a favorite of mine from a young age.) Many of the other stories, however, you probably will not have come across before. They encompass a wide time span,

7

from the medieval French legend of the Werewolf (retold here with beautiful simplicity and elegance by Barbara Leonie Picard) to my own story, "Howl", whose ink (or should I say blood) is barely dry on the page.

With the exception of one or two, all are tales of terror, though they may invoke other reactions too: revulsion perhaps, excitement, wonder, shock, even pity. It's hard not to feel compassion for the ghostly vampire in August Derleth's "The Drifting Snow", and I defy anyone not to be moved by the resolution of Jane Yolen's haunting story, "Mama Gone". On a lighter note, one or two of the stories – Woody Allen's spoof "Count Dracula" and William F. Nolan's fang-in-cheek "Getting Dead" – will, I hope, make you laugh.

As an author who writes about adolescence, I'm particularly intrigued by the theme of transformation that is such an essential part of this genre. Vampires and werewolves are changing beings and this is an important element of their appeal. I see in these metamorphoses a parallel with the physical and emotional changes of adolescence. These links are certainly present in Richard Matheson's spine-tingling story, "Drink My Blood" – while the young, newly inheriting Earl in "The Horror at Chilton Castle" has to endure a horrific rites-of-passage ritual you wouldn't wish on your worst enemy.

The stories I have chosen are very different in style, content and narrative viewpoint, but what I like about them all is the fine quality of the writing and the compelling nature of the storytelling. Sometimes in just a few pages, as with Angela Carter's "The Werewolf", and at other times at greater length, as with Carl Jacobi's "Revelations in Black", these tales cast a powerful, spellbinding magic. All, I believe, are truly memorable and I commend each of them to you. May they curdle your blood and chill you to the bone . . .

Alan Durant,
May 1998

# DRACULA

*BRAM STOKER*

### DR. SEWARD'S DIARY *(continued)*

IT WAS JUST A QUARTER before twelve o'clock when we got into the churchyard over the low wall. The night was dark, with occasional gleams of moonlight between the rents of the heavy clouds that scudded across the sky. We all kept somehow close together, with Van Helsing slightly in front as he led the way. When we had come close to the tomb I looked well at Arthur, for I feared that the proximity to a place laden with so sorrowful a memory would upset him; but he bore himself well. I took it that the very mystery of the proceeding tended in some way to counteract his grief. The Professor unlocked the door, and seeing a natural hesitation among us for various reasons, solved the difficulty by entering first himself. The rest of us followed, and he closed the door. He then lit a dark lantern and pointed to the coffin. Arthur stepped forward, hesitatingly; Van Helsing said to me:

"You were with me here yesterday. Was the body of Miss Lucy in that coffin?"

"It was." The Professor turned to the rest, saying:

"You hear, and yet there is one who does not believe with me." He took his screwdriver and again took off the lid of the coffin. Arthur looked on, very pale but silent; when the lid was removed he stepped forward. He evidently did not know that there was a leaden coffin, or, at any rate, had not thought of it. When he saw the rent in the lead, the blood rushed to his face for an instant, but as quickly fell away again, so that he remained of a ghastly whiteness; he was still silent. Van Helsing forced back the leaden flange, and we all looked in and recoiled.

The coffin was empty!

For several minutes, no one spoke a word. The silence was broken by Quincey Morris:

"Professor, I answered for you. Your word is all I want. I wouldn't ask such a thing ordinarily—I wouldn't so dishonor you as to imply a doubt; but this is a mystery that goes beyond any honor or dishonor. Is this your doing?"

"I swear to you by all that I hold sacred that I have not removed nor touched her. What happened was this: Two nights ago, my friend Seward and I came here—with good purpose, believe me. I opened that coffin, which was then sealed up, and we found it, as now, empty. We then waited, and saw something white come through the trees. The next day we came here in daytime, and she lay there. Did she not, friend John?"

"Yes."

"That night, we were just in time. One more so small child was missing, and we find it, thank God, unharmed among the graves. Yesterday, I came here before sundown, for at sundown the Un-Dead can move. I waited here all the night till the sun rose, but I saw nothing. It was most probable that it was because I had laid over the clamps of those doors garlic, which the Un-Dead cannot bear, and other things which they shun. Last night there was no exodus, so tonight before the sundown, I took away my garlic and other things. And so it is we find this coffin empty. But bear with me. So far there is much that is strange. Wait you with me outside, unseen and unheard, and things much stranger are yet to be. So"—here he shut the dark slide of his lantern—"now to the outside." He opened the door, and we filed out, he coming last and locking the door behind him.

Oh! but it seemed fresh and pure in the night air after the terror of that vault. How sweet it was to see the clouds race by, and the brief gleams of the moonlight between the scudding clouds crossing and passing—like the gladness and sorrow of a man's life; how sweet it was to breathe the fresh air, that had no taint of death and decay; how humanizing to see the red lighting of the sky beyond the hill, and to hear far away the muffled roar that marks the life of a great city. Each in his own way was solemn and overcome. Arthur was silent, and was, I could see, striving to grasp the purpose and the inner meaning of the mystery. I was myself tolerably patient, and half inclined again to throw aside doubt and to accept Van Helsing's conclusions. Quincey Morris was phlegmatic in the way of a man who accepts all things, and accepts them in the spirit of cool bravery, with hazard of all he has to stake. Not being able to smoke, he cut himself a good-sized plug of tobacco, and began to chew. As to Van Helsing, he was employed in a definite way. First he took from his bag a mass of what looked like thin, waferlike biscuit, which was carefully rolled up in a white napkin; next he took out a double-handful of some whitish stuff, like dough or putty. He crumbled the wafer up fine and worked it into the mass between his hands. This he then took, and rolling it into thin strips, began to lay them into the crevices between the door and its setting in the tomb. I was somewhat puzzled at this, and being close, asked him what it was that he was doing. Arthur and Quincey drew near also, as they too were curious. He answered:

"I am closing the tomb, so that the Un-Dead may not enter."

"And is that stuff you have put there going to do it?" asked Quincey. "Great Scott! Is this a game?"

"It is."

"What is that which you are using?" This time the question was by Arthur. Van Helsing reverently lifted his hat as he answered:

"The Host. I brought it from Amsterdam. I have an Indulgence." It was an answer that appalled the most skeptical of us, and we felt individually that in the presence of such earnest purpose as the Professor's, a purpose which could thus use the to him most sacred of things, it was impossible to distrust. In respectful silence we took the places assigned to us close around the tomb, but hidden from the sight of anyone approaching. I pitied the others, especially Arthur. I had myself been apprenticed by my former visits to this watching horror; and yet I, who had up to an hour ago repudiated the proofs, felt my heart sink within me. Never did tombs look so ghastly white; never did cypress, or yew, or juniper so seem the embodiment of funereal gloom; never did tree or grass wave or rustle so ominously; never did bough creak so mysteriously; and never did the far-away howling of dogs send such a woeful presage through the night.

There was a long spell of silence, a big, aching void, and then from the Professor a keen "S-s-s-s!" He pointed; and far down the avenue of yews we saw a white figure advance—a dim white figure, which held something dark at its breast. The figure stopped, and at the moment a ray of moonlight fell between the masses of driving clouds and showed in startling prominence a dark-haired woman, dressed in the cerements of the grave. We could not see the face, for it was bent down over what we saw to be a fair-haired child. There was a pause and a sharp little cry, such as a child gives in sleep, or a dog as it lies before the fire and dreams. We were starting forward, but the Professor's warning hand, seen by us as he stood behind a yew tree, kept us back; and then, as we looked, the white figure moved forward again. It was now near enough for us to see clearly, and the moonlight still held. My own heart grew cold as ice, and I could hear the gasp of Arthur as we recognized the features of Lucy Westenra. Lucy Westenra, but yet how changed. The sweetness was turned to adamantine, heartless cruelty, and the purity to voluptuous

12

wantonness. Van Helsing stepped out, and, obedient to his gesture, we all advanced too; the four of us ranged in a line before the door of the tomb. Van Helsing raised his lantern and drew the slide; by the concentrated light that fell on Lucy's face we could see that the lips were crimson with fresh blood, and that the stream had trickled over her chin and stained the purity of her lawn death-robe.

We shuddered with horror. I could see by the tremulous light that even Van Helsing's iron nerve had failed. Arthur was next to me, and if I had not seized his arm and held him up, he would have fallen.

When Lucy—I call the thing that was before us Lucy because it bore her shape—saw us she drew back with an angry snarl, such as a cat gives when taken unaware; then her eyes ranged over us. Lucy's eyes in form and color; but Lucy's eyes unclean and full of hell-fire, instead of the pure, gentle orbs we knew. At that moment, the remnant of my love passed into hate and loathing; had she then to be killed, I could have done it with savage delight. As she looked, her eyes blazed with unholy light, and the face became wreathed with a voluptuous smile. Oh, God, how it made me shudder to see it! With a careless motion, she flung to the ground, callous as a devil, the child that up to now she had clutched strenuously to her breast, growling over it as a dog growls over a bone. The child gave a sharp cry, and lay there moaning. There was a cold-bloodedness in the act which wrung a groan from Arthur; when she advanced to him with outstretched arms and a wanton smile, he fell back and hid his face in his hands.

She still advanced, however, and with a languorous, voluptuous grace, said:

"Come to me, Arthur. Leave these others and come to me. My arms are hungry for you. Come, and we can rest together. Come, my husband, come!"

There was something diabolically sweet in her tones— something of the tingling of glass when struck—which rang through the brains even of us who heard the words addressed to another. As for Arthur, he seemed under a spell; moving his hands from his face, he opened wide his arms. She was leaping for them, when Van Helsing sprang forward and held between them his little golden crucifix. She recoiled from it, and, with a suddenly distorted face, full of rage, dashed past him as if to enter the tomb.

When within a foot or two of the door, however, she stopped as if arrested by some irresistible force. Then she turned, and her face was shown in the clear burst of moonlight and by the lamp, which had now no quiver from Van Helsing's iron nerves. Never did I see such baffled malice on a face; and never, I trust, shall such ever be seen again by mortal eyes. The beautiful color became livid, the eyes seemed to throw out sparks of hell-fire, the brows were wrinkled as though the folds of the flesh were the coils of Medusa's snakes, and the lovely, bloodstained mouth grew to an open square, as in the passion masks of the Greeks and Japanese. If ever a face meant death—if looks could kill—we saw it at that moment.

And so for full half-a-minute, which seemed an eternity, she remained between the lifted crucifix and the sacred closing of her means of entry. Van Helsing broke the silence by asking Arthur:

"Answer me, o my friend! Am I to proceed in my work?"

Arthur threw himself on his knees, and hid his face in his hands, as he answered:

"Do as you will, friend; do as you will. There can be no horror like this ever, any more!" and he groaned in spirit. Quincey and I simultaneously moved toward him, and took his arms. We could hear the click of the closing lantern as Van Helsing held it down; coming close to the tomb, he began to remove from the chinks some of the sacred emblem which he had placed there. We all looked on in horrified amazement as we saw, when he stood back, the woman, with a corporeal body as real at the moment as our own, pass in through the interstice where scarce a knife blade could have gone. We all felt a glad sense of relief when we saw the Professor calmly

restoring the strings of putty to the edges of the door.

When this was done, he lifted the child and said:

"Come now, my friends; we can do no more till tomorrow. There is a funeral at noon, so here we shall all come before long after that. The friends of the dead will all be gone by two, and when the sexton locks the gate, we shall remain. Then there is more to do, but not like this of tonight. As for this little one, he is not much harmed, and by tomorrow night he shall be well. We shall leave him where the police will find him, as on the other night; and then to home." Coming close to Arthur, he said:

"My friend Arthur, you have had sore trial; but after, when you will look back, you will see how it was necessary. You are now in the bitter waters, my child. By this time tomorrow, you will, please God, have passed them, and have drunk of the sweet waters; so do not mourn overmuch. Till then I shall not ask you to forgive me."

Arthur and Quincey came home with me, and we tried to cheer each other on the way. We had left the child in safety, and were tired, so we all slept with more or less reality of sleep.

*September 29, night.* A little before twelve o'clock we three—Arthur, Quincey Morris, and myself—called for the Professor. It was odd to notice that, by common consent, we had all put on black clothes. Of course, Arthur wore black, for he was in deep mourning, but the rest of us wore it by instinct. We got to the churchyard by half-past one, and strolled about, keeping out of official observation, so that when the gravediggers had completed their task, and the sexton, under the belief that everyone had gone, had locked the gate, we had the place all to ourselves. Van Helsing, instead of his little black bag, had with him a long leather one, something like a cricketing bag; it was manifestly of fair weight.

When we were alone and had heard the last of the footsteps die out up the road, we silently, and as if by ordered intention, followed the Professor to the tomb. He unlocked the door, and we entered, closing it behind us. Then he took from his bag the lantern, which he lit, and also two wax candles, which, when lighted, he stuck by melting their own ends, on other coffins, so that they might give light sufficient to work by. When he again lifted the lid off Lucy's coffin, we all looked— Arthur trembling like an aspen—and saw that the body lay there in all its death-beauty. But there was no love in my own heart, nothing but loathing for the foul Thing which had taken Lucy's shape without her soul. I could see even Arthur's face grow hard as he looked. Presently he said to Van Helsing:

"Is this really Lucy's body, or only a demon in her shape?"

"It is her body, and yet not it. But wait a while, and you shall see her as she was, and is."

She seemed like a nightmare of Lucy as she lay there; the pointed teeth, the bloodstained, voluptuous mouth—which it made one shudder to see—the whole carnal and unspiritual appearance, seeming like a devilish mockery of Lucy's sweet purity. Van Helsing, in his methodical manner, began taking the various contents from his bag and placing them ready for use. First he took out a soldering iron and some plumbing solder, and then a small oil lamp, which gave out, when lit in a corner of the tomb, gas which burned at fierce heat with a blue flame; then his operating knives, which he placed to hand, and last a round wooden stake, some two-and-a-half or three-inches thick and about three-feet long. One end of it was hardened by charring in the fire, and was sharpened to a fine point. With this stake came a heavy hammer, such as in households is used in the coal cellar for breaking the lumps. To me, a doctor's preparations for work of any kind are stimulating and bracing, but the effect of these things on both Arthur and Quincey was to cause them a sort of consternation. They both, however, kept their courage, and remained silent and quiet.

When all was ready, Van Helsing said:

"Before we do anything, let me tell you this; it is out of the lore and experience of the ancients and of all those who have studied the powers of the Un-Dead. When they become such, there comes with the change the curse of immortality; they cannot die, but must go on age after age adding new victims and multiplying the evils of the world; for all that die from the preying of the Un-Dead become themselves Un-Dead, and prey on their kind. And so the circle goes on ever widening, like as the ripples from a stone thrown in the water. Friend Arthur, if you had met that kiss which you know of before poor Lucy die; or again, last night when you open your arms to her, you would in time, when you had died, have become *nosferatu*, as they call it in Eastern Europe, and would all time make more of those Un-Deads that so have filled us with horror. The career of this so unhappy dear lady is but just begun. Those children whose blood she suck are not as yet so much the worse; but if she live on, Un-Dead, more and more they lose their blood, and by her power over them they come to her; and so she draw their blood with that so wicked mouth. But if she die in truth, then all cease; the tiny wounds of the throats disappear, and they go back to their plays unknowing ever of what has been. But of the most blessed of all, when this now Un-Dead be made to rest as true dead, then the soul of the poor lady whom we love shall again be free. Instead of working wickedness by night, and growing more debased in the assimilation of it by day, she shall take her place with the other Angels. So that, my friend, it will be a blessed hand for her that shall strike the blow that sets her free. To this I am willing, but is there none among us who has a better right? Will it be no joy to think of hereafter in the silence of the night when sleep is not: "It was my hand that sent her to the stars; it was the hand of him that loved her best, the hand that of all she would herself have chosen, had it been to her to choose? Tell me if there be such a one among us."

We all looked at Arthur. He saw, too, what we all did, the infinite kindness which suggested that his should be the hand which would restore Lucy to us as a holy, and not an unholy, memory; he stepped forward and said bravely, though his hand trembled, and his face was as pale as snow:

"My true friend, from the bottom of my broken heart, I thank you. Tell me what I am to do, and I shall not falter!" Van

Helsing laid a hand on his shoulder, and said:

"Brave lad! A moment's courage, and it is done. This stake must be driven through her. It will be a fearful ordeal—be not deceived in that—but it will be only a short time, and you will then rejoice more than your pain was great; from this grim tomb you will emerge as though you tread on air. But you must not falter when once you have begun. Only think that we, your true friends, are round you, and that we pray for you all the time."

"Go on," said Arthur hoarsely. "Tell me what I am to do."

"Take this stake in your left hand, ready to place the point over the heart, and the hammer in your right. Then when we begin our prayer for the dead—I shall read him; I have here the book, and the others shall follow—strike in God's name, that so all may be well with the dead that we love, and that the Un-Dead pass away."

Arthur took the stake and the hammer, and when once his mind was set on action; his hands never trembled nor even quivered. Van Helsing opened his missal and began to read, and Quincey and I followed as well as we could. Arthur placed the point over the heart, and as I looked I could see its dint in the white flesh. Then he struck with all his might.

The Thing in the coffin writhed; and a hideous, blood-curdling screech came from the opened red lips. The body shook and quivered and twisted in wild contortions; the sharp white teeth champed together till the lips were cut and the mouth was smeared with a crimson foam. But Arthur never faltered. He looked like a figure of Thor as his untrembling arm rose and fell, driving deeper and deeper the mercy-bearing stake, while the blood from the pierced heart welled and spurted up around it. His face was set, and high duty seemed to shine through it; the sight of it gave us courage, so that our voices seemed to ring through the little vault.

And then the writhing and quivering of the body became less, and the teeth ceased to champ, and the face to quiver. Finally it lay still. The terrible task was over.

The hammer fell from Arthur's hand. He reeled and would have fallen had we not caught him. Great drops of sweat sprang out on his forehead, and his breath came in broken gasps. It had indeed been an awful strain on him; and had he not been forced to his task by more than human considerations, he could never have gone through with it. For a few minutes we were so taken up with him that we did not look toward the coffin. When we did, however, a murmur of startled surprise ran from one to the other of us. We gazed so eagerly that Arthur rose, for he had been seated on the ground, and came and looked too, and then a glad, strange light broke over his face, and dispelled altogether the gloom of horror that lay upon it.

There in the coffin lay no longer the foul Thing that we had so dreaded and grown to hate that the work of her destruction was yielded as a privilege to the one best entitled to it, but Lucy as we had seen her in her life, with her face of unequalled sweetness and purity. True that there were there, as we had seen them in life, the traces of care and pain and waste; but these were all dear to us, for they marked her truth to what we knew. One and all, we felt that the holy calm that lay like sunshine over the wasted face and form was only an earthly token and symbol of the calm that was to reign forever.

Van Helsing came and laid his hand on Arthur's shoulder, and said to him:

"And now, Arthur, my friend, dear lad, am I not forgiven?"

The reaction of the terrible strain came as he took the old man's hand in his, and raising it to his lips, pressed it, saying:

"Forgiven! God bless you that you have given my dear one her soul again, and me peace." He put his hands on the Professor's shoulder, and laying his head on his breast, cried for a while silently, while we stood unmoving. When he raised his head, Van Helsing said to him:

"And now, my child, you may kiss her. Kiss her dead lips if you will, as she would have you do, if for her to choose. For she is not a grinning devil now—not any more a foul Thing for all eternity. No longer she is the devil's Un-Dead. She is God's true dead, whose soul is with Him!"

Arthur bent and kissed her, and then we sent him and Quincey out of the tomb; the Professor and I sawed the top off the stake, leaving the point of it in the body. Then we cut off the head, and filled the mouth with garlic. We soldered up the leaden coffin, screwed on the coffin lid, and gathering up our belongings, came away. When the Professor locked the door, he gave the key to Arthur.

Outside the air was sweet, the sun shone, and the birds sang, and it seemed as if all nature were tuned to a different pitch. There was gladness and mirth and peace everywhere, for we were at rest ourselves on one account, and we were glad, though it was with a tempered joy.

# THE WEREWOLF

*BARBARA LEONIE PICARD*

*A French legend*

THERE DWELT IN A CASTLE in Brittany a young Baron who was much beloved of his King, and a good friend he was to him. This Baron had a wife, very fair and sweet to look upon, but quite otherwise in her heart, for though she smiled on her lord and spoke loving words, she cared not for him; all her heart was given to another knight, and she longed only that she might be rid of her lord and wedded to that other.

For three days out of every seven, the Baron would be absent from his castle, and neither his lady nor any of his followers knew where he went or what he did during that time. The lady thought long on this and wondered how she might turn it to her advantage. One day, with many smiles and caresses, she said, "There is a favor I would ask of you, dear lord."

The Baron smiled. "There is nothing I can deny you, as well you know," he said.

"Then do not leave me for three days out of every week, for I am lonely when you are gone."

The Baron turned away from her; he was no longer smiling and his voice was troubled. "I would stay with you if I could. But alas, I cannot."

"Tell me where you go," she said. But he would not. Yet she coaxed and pleaded, weeping and protesting that he could not love her if he did not tell her; so that at last he could bear it no longer, and swearing her to secrecy, he said, "Through no will of my own, I am a werewolf. Three days out of every seven must I spend as a wolf, running wild through the forest, a savage beast."

"How does this change take place?" asked his lady.

"In the forest, I put off my garments and lay them where I may find them again, and then I become a wolf. But when the three days are passed, I clothe myself and I am a man once more."

Cunningly she asked, "Dear lord, where do you hide your garments when you are becoming a wolf?"

"That, dearest, may I never tell to anyone, for if I could not find them when the three days were done, then I should have to remain as a wolf forever, or until my garments were restored to me."

Inwardly, she rejoiced when she heard this, and from that moment gave him no peace, forever asking him the same question and swearing that it was for his own good that she asked; and because he trusted her and believed her true, he told her, at last. "In the forest stands a ruined chapel, and near by, hidden by a bush, is a hollow stone. There do I hide my garments."

His lady kissed him and said she was proud to know how much he trusted her, and she swore his secret would come to no harm with her.

But the very next time that the Baron left his castle to go to the forest alone, she sent for the knight whom she loved and told him all. And she bade him go to the hollow stone by the ruined chapel and bring away her husband's garments. Greatly rejoicing, the knight did so, and she hid them in a coffer.

When the three days were passed, and the Baron in his wolf guise came to the hollow stone and found his garments gone, he knew his lady had betrayed him; but there was nothing that he might do to help himself, for if he but showed himself beyond the edge of the forest, men would loose hounds on him, and come against him with stones and cudgels, so that his life was likely to be quickly lost if he did not remain in the shelter of the trees.

When the weeks passed and the Baron did not come home, his lady wept a little and exclaimed a lot about the faithlessness of the lord who had abandoned her; and then she was married to the knight she loved, well pleased with the way things had gone.

But the wolf roamed in the forest, slaying and devouring after the manner of wolves, and ever grieving, until a year had passed, and one day the King chanced to hunt in that forest. The hounds came upon the tracks of the wolf and, baying and impatient, they followed him. All day the hounds trailed the wolf through the forest with the King and his courtiers close after them, and in the evening, the wolf, weary and torn by the thorns and the brambles, could go no farther, and he turned at bay, sure that his end had come. Then suddenly, beyond the ring of panting hounds, the bared fangs and the lolling tongues and the eager eyes, he saw the young King who had once been his friend. With his remaining strength he fought his way through the hounds, and running to the King, placed one paw upon the King's stirrup and laid his head upon the King's foot. Growling, the hounds came after him, but the King, much moved, beat them off and called to his companions to leash them.

"This poor wild creature has asked my mercy," said the King. "He shall have it. Let us go and leave him free in the forest." And he turned and rode for his castle. Yet the wolf would not leave him, but limped along painfully beside his horse, even to the castle gates, so that all who saw marveled at it. "He has asked my protection," said the King. "He shall have it for so long as he pleases." And he forbade anyone to harm the wolf and ordered fresh meat to be provided for him daily. And for his part, the wolf harmed no one in the castle, being ever gentle with everyone, and he followed the King like a dog; for had the courtiers not once been his companions in the jousting and on the tourney-ground, and had the King not been his friend? By day the wolf was always at the King's side, and at night he slept at the foot of his bed; and the King took more delight in his wolf than in any of his hounds.

Soon after, the King called all his vassals to court, and there he took counsel with them, and after, feasted them richly. Now, among those who were summoned was that same knight who had married the Baron's false lady, and when he and his followers came before the King, the wolf growled and leaped upon him, throwing him to the ground, and was restrained from doing him great hurt only with difficulty by those who stood around. The King was surprised, for until that moment the wolf had harmed no man. Yet it happened not once, but three times that he leaped upon the knight and was beaten off by the knight's friends; so that from fear that the knight or the wolf might be harmed, the King was forced to keep the wolf chained until the knight was gone from the castle, which he was glad to do as soon as he might, wondering much and not a little fearful.

It chanced, a few months later, that the King hunted again in the forest where he had found the wolf, and he lay for the night in a hunting-lodge on the edge of the forest close by the lands and the castle that had belonged to the Baron. The Baron's false lady, wishing to win favor for herself and her knight, rode in the morning from the castle, richly attended and bearing gifts for the King. But no sooner had she come into the presence of the King than the wolf gave a great howl and leaped at her throat, so that she cried out in fear. In an instant, every man there save the King had drawn his dagger and hastened to defend the lady, and the wolf would surely have been slain, had the King not cried out to prevent it.

Then the King, holding the wolf close in his arms, so that he could neither be harmed nor do harm, said slowly, "This is the

lady who was wife to that Baron who was once my friend and who went no man knows where. And the knight whom my wolf attacked, he is the second lord of this lady and now rules the lands which were once my friend's." And he ordered the lady and her knight to be bound, and they were locked away in a dungeon. And there in the cold and the darkness, with little to drink and less to eat, the lady in her terror confessed her crime and told where she had hidden the Baron's garments.

Immediately, the King sent for them, and when they were brought, he laid them before the wolf, while all watched to see what might happen. But the wolf looked at the garments and made no move.

"He is no more than a wolf," said the courtiers. "The good Baron is lost to us forever."

But the King said gently, "It would be a great shame to a knight to turn from a wolf to a man before the eyes of so many." And he rose and took up the garments and went to his own bedchamber with the wolf following him, and he laid the garments on the bed and came out from the room alone, locking the door behind him. After a little while he called two others and they went together to the bedchamber. The King unlocked the door and they entered, and there on the King's bed lay the Baron, asleep. And no man could have been happier than the King in that moment.

The false lady and her knight were driven forth from the kingdom, and the Baron regained his castle and his lands. But most of his time he spent, whether as a wolf or as a man, at the court of the King.

# THE VAMPIRE OF KALDENSTEIN

*FREDERICK COWLES*

## I

SINCE I WAS A LAD, I have been accustomed to spending my vacations wandering about the more remote parts of Europe. I have had some pleasant times in Italy, Spain, Norway, and southern France, but of all the countries I have explored in this fashion, Germany is my favorite. It is an ideal vacationland for the lover of open-air life whose means are small and tastes simple, for the people are always so friendly and the inns are good and cheap. I have had many excellent vacations in Germany, but one will always stand out in my memory because of a very strange and remarkable experience which befell me.

It was in the summer of 1933, and I had practically made up my mind to go on a cruise to the Canaries with Donald Young. Then he caught a very childish complaint—the measles, in fact—and I was left to make my own arrangements. The idea of joining an organized cruise without a companion did not appeal to me. I am not a particularly sociable kind of person, and these cruises seem to be one round of dances, cocktail parties, and bridge drives.

I was afraid of feeling like a fish out of water, so I decided to forgo the cruise. Instead I got out my maps of Germany and began to plan a walking tour.

Half the fun of a vacation is in the planning of it, and I suppose I decided on a particular part of the country and changed my mind half a dozen times. At first I liked the Moselle Valley, then it was the Lahn. I toyed with the idea of the Black Forest, swung over to the Harz Mountains, and then thought it might be fun to re-visit Saxony. Finally, I fixed upon southern Bavaria, because I had never been there and it seemed better to break fresh ground.

Two days of third-class travel is tiring even for a hardened globe-trotter, and I arrived at Munich feeling thoroughly weary and sore. By some good chance I discovered the Inn of the Golden Apple, near the Hofgarten, where Peter Schmidt sells both good wine and good food, and has a few rooms for the accommodation of guests. Peter, who lived in Canada for ten years and speaks excellent English, knew exactly how I was feeling. He gave me a comfortable room for one mark a night, served me with hot coffee and rolls, and advised me to go to bed and stay there until I was completely rested. I took his advice, slept soundly for twelve hours, and awakened feeling as fresh as a daisy. A dish of roast pork and two glasses of lager beer completed the cure, and I sallied forth to see something of Munich.

The city is the fourth largest in Germany and has much of interest to show the visitor. The day was well advanced, but I managed to inspect the Frauen-Kirche with its fine stained glass, the old Rathaus, and the fourteenth-century church of St. Peter, near the Marien-Platz. I looked in at the Regina-Palast, where a tea dance was in progress, and then went back to the Golden Apple for dinner. Afterward, I attended a performance of *Die Meistersinger* at the National Theater. It was past midnight when I retired to bed, and by then I had decided to stay in Munich for another day.

I won't bore you with a description of the things I saw and did on that second day. It was just the usual round of sights with nothing out of the ordinary.

After dinner Peter helped me to plan my tour. He revealed a very intimate knowledge of the Bavarian villages, and gave me a list of inns which eventually proved invaluable. It was he who suggested I should take a train to Rosenheim and begin my walk from there. We mapped out a route covering about two hundred miles and bringing me back to Munich at the end of fifteen days.

Well, to cut a long story short, I caught the early morning train to Rosenheim, and a deadly slow journey it was. It took nearly three hours to cover a distance of forty-six miles. The town itself is quite a cheerful place of the small industrial type, with a fifteenth-century church and a good museum of Bavarian paintings housed in an old chapel.

I did not linger there, but started off along the road to Traunstein—a pleasant road curving around the Chiem-See, the largest lake in Bavaria.

I spent the night at Traunstein and the next day pushed on to the old walled town of Mühldorf. From there I planned to make for Vilshofen by way of Pfarrkirchen. But I took a wrong turning and found myself in a small place called Gangkofen. The local innkeeper tried to be helpful and directed me to a field path which he said would prove a short cut to Pfarrkirchen. Evidently I misunderstood his instructions, for evening came and I was hopelessly lost in the heart of a range of low hills which were not marked on my map. Darkness was falling when I came upon a small village huddled under the shadow of a high cliff upon which stood a gray, stone castle.

Fortunately, the village possessed an inn—a primitive place but moderately comfortable. The landlord was an intelligent kind of chap and friendly enough, although he informed me that visitors were seldom seen in the district. The name of the hamlet was Kaldenstein.

I was served with a simple meal of goat's-milk cheese, salad, coarse bread, and a bottle of thin red wine, and, having done justice to the spread, went for a short stroll.

The moon had risen and the castle stood out against a

cloudless sky like some magic castle in a fairy tale. It was only a small building—square, with four turrets—but it was the most romantic-looking fortress I had ever seen. A light twinkled in one of the windows, so I knew the place was inhabited. A steep path and a flight of steps cut in the rock led up to it, and I half considered paying the Lord of Kaldenstein a late visit. Instead I returned to the inn and joined the few men who were drinking in the public room.

The company was mainly composed of folk of the laboring class, and although they were polite they had little of that friendly spirit one is accustomed to meet with in German villages. They seemed morose and unresponsive and I had the impression that they shared some dread secret. I did my best to engage them in conversation without success. Then, to get one of them to speak, I asked, "Tell me, my friends, who lives in the castle on the hillside?"

The effect of the harmless question upon them was startling. Those who were drinking placed their beer mugs on the table and gazed at me with consternation on their faces. Some made the sign of the cross, and one old chap hoarsely whispered, "Silence, stranger. God forbid that he should hear."

My inquiry seemed to have upset them altogether, and within ten minutes they all left in a group. I apologized to the landlord for any indiscretion I had been guilty of, and hoped my presence had not robbed him of custom.

He waved aside my excuses and assured me that the men would not have stayed long in any case.

"They are terrified of any mention of the castle," he said, "and consider it unlucky to even glance at the building after nightfall."

"But why?" I inquired. "Who lives there?"

"It is the home of Count Ludwig von Kaldenstein."

"And how long has he lived up there?" I asked.

The man moved over to the door and carefully shut and barred it before he replied. Then he came over to my chair and whispered, "He has been up there for nearly three hundred years."

"Nonsense," I exclaimed laughing. "How can any man, be he count or peasant, live for three hundred years. I suppose you mean that his family has held the castle for that length of time?"

"I mean exactly what I say, young man," answered the old fellow earnestly. "The Count's family has held the castle for ten centuries, and the Count himself has dwelt in Burg Kaldenstein for nearly three hundred years."

"But how can that be possible?"

"He is a vampire. Deep down in the castle rock are great vaults and in one of these the Count sleeps during the day so that the sunlight may not touch him. Only at night does he walk outside."

This was too fantastic for anything. I am afraid I smiled in a skeptical manner, but the poor landlord was obviously very serious, and I hesitated to make another remark that might wound his feelings. I finished my beer and got up to go to bed. As I was mounting the stairs my host called me back, and, grasping my arm, said, "Please, sir, let me beg you to keep your window closed. The night air of Kaldenstein is not healthy."

On reaching my room I found the window already tightly shut, although the atmosphere was like that of an oven. Of course, I opened it at once and leaned out to fill my lungs with fresh air. The window looked directly upon the castle and, in the clear light of the full moon, the building appeared more than ever like some dream of fairyland.

I was just drawing back into the room when I thought I saw a black figure silhouetted against the sky on the summit of one of the turrets. Even as I watched, it flapped enormous wings and soared into the night. It seemed too large for an eagle, but the moonlight has an odd trick of distorting shapes. I watched until it was only a tiny, black speck in the far distance. Just then, from far away, a dog howled weirdly and mournfully.

Within a few moments I was ready for bed, and disregarding the innkeeper's warning, I left the window open. I took my electric flashlight from my rucksack and placed it on the small bedside table—a table above which hung a wooden crucifix.

I am usually asleep as soon as my head touches the pillow, but on this particular night I found it difficult to settle. The moonlight disturbed me and I tossed about, vainly trying to get comfortable. I counted sheep until I was heartily sick of imagining the silly creatures passing through a gap in a hedge, but still sleep eluded me.

A clock in the house chimed the hour of midnight, and suddenly I had the unpleasant feeling that I was no longer alone. For a moment I felt frightened and then, overcoming my fear, I turned over. There, by the window and black against the moonlight, was the figure of a tall man. I started up in bed and groped for my flashlight. In doing so I knocked something from the wall. It was the little crucifix and my fingers closed over it almost as soon as it touched the table. From the direction of the window came a muttered curse, and I saw the figure poise itself on the sill and spring out into the night. In that brief moment I noticed one other thing—the man, whoever he was, cast no shadow. The moonlight seemed to stream right through him.

It must have been almost half an hour before I dared get out of bed and close the window. After that, I fell asleep immediately and slept soundly until the maid called me at eight o'clock.

In the broad daylight the events of the night seemed too ridiculous to be true, and I decided that I had been the victim of some fantastic nightmare. In answer to the landlord's polite inquiry, I vowed I had spent a most comfortable night, although I am afraid my looks must have belied the statement.

## II

After breakfast, I went out to explore the village. It was rather larger than it had appeared on the previous evening, with some of the houses lying in a valley at the side of the road.

There was even a small church, Romanesque in type and sadly in need of repair. I entered the building and was inspecting its gaudy high altar when a priest came in through a side door. He was a lean, ascetic-looking man, and at once gave me a friendly greeting. I returned his salutation and told him I was from England. He apologized for the obvious poverty of the building, pointed out some good fifteenth-century glass, a carved font of the same period, and a very pleasing statue of the Madonna.

Later, as I stood at the church door with him, I looked toward the castle and said, "I wonder, Father, if the Lord of Kaldenstein will give me a welcome as friendly as the one I have received from you?"

"The Lord of Kaldenstein," repeated the priest with a tremor in his voice. "Surely you are not proposing to visit the castle?"

"That is my intention," I replied. "It looks a very interesting place and I should be sorry to leave this part of the world without seeing it."

"Let me implore you not to attempt to enter that accursed place," he pleaded. "Visitors are not welcomed at Kaldenstein Castle. Besides that," he went on with a change in his voice, "there is nothing to see in the building."

"What about the wonderful vaults in the cliff and the man who has lived in them for three hundred years?" I laughed.

The priest's face visibly blanched. "Then you know of the vampire," he said. "Do not laugh at evil, my son. May God preserve us all from the living dead." He made the sign of the Cross.

"But Father," I cried, "surely you do not believe in such a medieval superstition?"

"Every man believes what he knows to be true, and we of Kaldenstein can prove that no burial has taken place in the castle since 1645, when Count Feodor died and his cousin Ludwig from Hungary inherited the estate."

"Such a tale is too absurd," I remonstrated. "There must be some reasonable explanation of the mystery. It is unthinkable that a man who came to this place in 1645 can still be alive."

"Much is possible to those who serve the Devil," answered the priest. "Always throughout the history of the world, evil has warred with good, and often triumphed. Kaldenstein Castle is the haunt of terrible, unnatural wickedness, and I urge you to keep as far away from it as you can."

He bade me a courteous farewell, lifted his hand in a gentle benediction, and re-entered the church.

Now I must confess that the priest's words gave me a most uncomfortable feeling and made me think of my nightmare. Had it been a dream after all? Or could it have been the vampire himself seeking to make me one of his victims, and only being frustrated in his plan by my accidental gripping of the crucifix? These thoughts passed through my mind and I almost abandoned my resolve to seek admittance to the castle. Then I looked up again at the gray old walls gleaming in the morning sunshine, and laughed at my fears. No mythical monster from the Middle Ages was going to frighten me away. The priest was just as superstitious as his ignorant parishioners.

Whistling a popular song, I made my way up the village street and was soon climbing the narrow path which led to the castle. As the ascent became steeper, the path gave place to a flight of steps which brought me onto a small plateau before the main door of the building. There was no sign of life about the place, but a ponderous bell hung before the entrance. I pulled a rusty chain and set the cracked thing jangling. The sound disturbed a colony of rooks in one of the turrets and started them chattering, but no human being appeared to answer my summons. Again, I set the bell ringing. This time the echoes had hardly died away when I heard bolts being withdrawn. The great door creaked on its hinges, and an old man stood blinking in the sunlight.

"Who comes to Castle Kaldenstein?" he asked in a curious high-pitched voice, and I could see that he was half-blind.

"I am an English visitor," I answered, "and would like to see the Count."

"His Excellency does not receive visitors," was the reply,

and the man made to close the door in my face.

"But is it not permitted that I should see over the castle?" I asked hurriedly. "I am interested in medieval fortresses and should be sorry to leave Kaldenstein without inspecting this splendid building."

The old fellow peered out at me, and in a hesitant voice said, "There is little to see, sir, and I am afraid you would only be wasting your time."

"Yet, I should appreciate the privilege of a brief visit," I argued, "and I am sure the Count would not object. I do assure you I shall not be a nuisance and I have no desire to disturb His Excellency's privacy."

"What is the hour?" asked the man.

I informed him that it was barely eleven o'clock. He muttered something about it being "safe while the sun is in the sky," and motioned me to enter. I found myself in a bare hall, hung with rotting tapestry and smelling of damp and decay. At the end of the room was a canopied dais surmounted by a coat of arms.

"This is the main hall of the castle," mumbled my guide, "and it has witnessed many great historic scenes in the days of the great lords of Kaldenstein. Here Frederic, the sixth Count, put out the eyes of twelve Italian hostages, and afterward had them driven over the edge of the cliff. Here Count August is said to have poisoned a prince of Wurttemburg, and then sat at a feast with the dead body."

He went on with his tales of foul and treacherous deeds, and it was evident that the counts of Kaldenstein must have been a very unsavory lot. From the main hall he conducted me into a number of smaller rooms filled with moldering furniture. His own quarters were in the north turret, but although he showed me over the whole building I saw no room in which his master could be. The old fellow opened every door without hesitation and it seemed that, except for himself, the castle was untenanted.

"But where is the Count's room?" I inquired as we returned to the main hall.

He looked confused for a moment, and then replied, "We have certain underground apartments, and His Excellency uses one as his bedchamber. You see he can rest there undisturbed."

I thought that any room in the building would give him the quietness he required, without having to seek peace in the bowels of the earth.

"And have you no private chapel?" I asked.

"The chapel is also below."

I intimated that I was interested in chapels, and should very much like to see an example of an underground place of worship. The old man made several excuses, but at last consented to show me the crypt. Taking an old-fashioned lantern from a shelf, he lit the candle in it, and, lifting a portion of the tapestry from the wall, opened a hidden door. A sickly odor of damp corruption swept up at us. Muttering to himself, he led the way down a flight of stone steps and along a passage hollowed in the rock. At the end of this was another door which admitted us to a large cavern furnished like a church. The place stank like a charnel house, and the feeble light of the lantern only intensified the gloom. My guide led me toward the chancel and, lifting the light, pointed out a particularly revolting painting of Lazarus rising from the dead which hung above the altar. I moved forward to examine it more closely, and found myself near another door.

"And what is beyond this?"

"Speak softly, sir," he implored. "It is the vault in which rest the mortal remains of the lords of Kaldenstein."

And while he was speaking, I heard a sound from beyond that barrier—a sigh, and the kind of noise that might be made by a person turning in his sleep.

I think the old servitor also heard it, for he grasped me with a trembling hand and led me out of the chapel. His flickering light went before me as I mounted the stairs, and I laughed sharply with relief as we stepped into the castle hall again. He gave me a quick look and said, "That is all, sir. You see there is little of interest in this old building."

I tried to press a five-mark piece into his hand, but he refused to accept it.

"Money is of no use to me, sir," he whispered. "I have nothing to spend it on, for I live with the dead. Give the coin to the priest in the village and ask him to say a mass for me if you will."

I promised it should be done as he desired and then, in some mad spirit of bravado, asked, "And when does the Count receive visitors?"

"My master never receives visitors," was the reply.

"But surely he is sometimes in the castle itself? He doesn't spend all his time in the vaults," I urged.

"Usually after nightfall he sits in the hall for an hour or so, and sometimes walks on the battlements."

"Then I shall be back tonight," I cried. "I owe it to His Excellency to pay my respects to him."

The old man turned in the act of unfastening the door, and fixing his dim eyes upon my face said, "Come not to Kaldenstein after the sun has set lest you find that which shall fill your heart with fear."

"Don't try to frighten me with any of your hobgoblins," I rudely replied. Then, raising my voice, I cried, "Tonight I shall wait upon the Count von Kaldenstein."

The servant flung the door wide and the sunlight streamed into the moldering building.

"If you come, he will be ready to receive you," he said, "and remember that if you enter the castle again, you do so of your own free will."

### III

By the time evening came, my courage had quite evaporated and I wished I had taken the priest's advice and left Kaldenstein. But there is a streak of obstinacy in my makeup and, having vowed to visit the castle again, nothing could turn me from my purpose. I waited until dusk had fallen, and, saying nothing to the innkeeper of my intentions, made my way up the steep path to the fortress. The moon had not yet risen and I had to use my flashlight on the steps. I rang the cracked bell and the door opened almost immediately. There stood the old servant bowing a welcome.

"His Excellency will see you, sir," he cried. "Enter Kaldenstein Castle—enter of your own free will."

For one second I hesitated. Something seemed to warn me to retreat while there was still time. Then I plucked up courage and stepped over the threshold.

A log fire was burning in the enormous grate and gave a more cheerful atmosphere to the gloomy apartment. Candles gleamed in the silver candelabra, and I saw that a man was sitting at the table on the dais. As I advanced, he came down to greet me.

How shall I describe the Count of Kaldenstein? He was unusually tall, with a face of unnatural pallor. His hair was intensely black, and his hands delicately shaped, but with very pointed fingers and long nails. His eyes impressed me most. As he crossed the room they seemed to glow with a red light, just as if the pupils were ringed with flame. However, his greeting was conventional enough.

"Welcome to my humble home, sir," he said, bowing very low. "I regret my inability to offer you a more hospitable welcome, but we live very frugally. It is seldom we entertain guests, and I am honored that you should take the trouble to call upon me."

I murmured some polite word of thanks, and he conducted me to a seat at the long table upon which stood a decanter and one glass.

"You will take wine?" he invited, and filled the glass to the brim. It was a rare old vintage, but I felt a little uncomfortable at having to drink alone.

"I trust you will excuse me for not joining you," he said, evidently noticing my hesitant manner. "I never drink wine." He smiled, and I saw that his front teeth were long and sharply pointed.

"And now tell me," he went on. "What are you doing in this part of the world? Kaldenstein is rather off the beaten track and we seldom see strangers."

I explained that I was on a walking tour and had missed my way to Pfarrkirchen. The Count laughed softly, and again showed his fanglike teeth.

"And so you came to Kaldenstein and of your own free will you have come to visit me."

I began to dislike these references to my free will. The expression seemed to be a kind of formula. The servant had used it when I was leaving after my morning visit, and again when he had admitted me that evening, and now the Count was making use of it.

"How else should I come but of my own free will?" I asked sharply.

"In the bad old days of the past, many have been brought to this castle by force. The only guests we welcome today are those who come willingly."

All this time a queer sensation was gradually coming over me; I felt as if all my energy was being sapped from me, and a deadly nausea was overpowering my senses. The Count went on uttering commonplaces, but his voice came from far away. I was conscious of his peculiar eyes gazing into mine. They grew larger and larger, and it seemed that I was looking into two wells of fire. And then, with a clumsy movement, I knocked my wine glass over. The frail thing shattered to fragments, and the noise restored me to my senses. A splinter pierced my hand and a tiny pool of blood formed on the table. I sought for a handkerchief, but before I could produce it I was terrified by an unearthly howl which echoed through the vaulted hall. The cry came from the lips of the Count, and in a moment he was bending over the blood on the table, licking it up with obvious relish. A more disgusting sight I have never witnessed, and, struggling to my feet, I made for the door.

But terror weakened my limbs, and the Count had overtaken me before I had covered many yards. His white hands grasped my arms and led me back to the chair I had vacated.

"My dear sir," he said. "I must beg you to excuse me for my

discourtesy. The members of my family have always been peculiarly affected by the sight of blood. Call it an idiosyncrasy if you like, but it does at times make us behave like wild animals. I am grieved to have so far forgotten my manners as to behave in such a strange way before a guest. I assure you that I have sought to conquer this failing, and for that reason I keep away from my fellow men."

The explanation seemed plausible enough, but it filled me with horror and loathing—more especially as I could see a tiny globule of blood clinging to his mouth.

"I fear I am keeping Your Excellency from bed," I suggested, "and in any case I think it is time I got back to the inn."

"Ah, no, my friend," he replied. "The night hours are the ones I enjoy best, and I shall be very grateful if you will remain with me until morning. The castle is a lonely place and your company will be a pleasant change. There is a room prepared for you in the south turret and tomorrow, who knows, there may be other guests to cheer us."

A deadly fear gripped my heart and I staggered to my feet stammering, "Let me go . . . Let me go. I must return to the village at once."

"You cannot return tonight, for a storm is brewing and the cliff path will be unsafe."

As he uttered these words he crossed to a window, and, flinging it open, raised one arm toward the sky. As if in obedience to his gesture, a flash of vivid lightning split the clouds, and a clap of thunder seemed to shake the castle. Then the rain came in a terrible deluge and a great wind howled across the mountains. The Count closed the casement and returned to the table.

"You see, my friend," he chuckled, "the very elements are against your return to the village. You must be satisfied with such poor hospitality as we can offer you, for tonight at any rate."

The red-rimmed eyes met mine, and again I felt my will being sapped from my body. His voice was no more than a whisper, and seemed to come from far away.

"Follow me, and I will conduct you to your room. You are my guest for tonight."

He took a candle from the table and, like a man in a trance, I followed him up a winding staircase, along an empty corridor, and into a cheerless room furnished with an ancient four-poster bed.

"Sleep well," he said with a wicked leer. "Tomorrow night you shall have other company."

The heavy door slammed behind him as he left me alone, and I heard a bolt being shot on the other side. Summoning what little strength was left in my body, I hurled myself against the door. It was securely fastened and I was a prisoner. Through the keyhole came the Count's purring voice.

"Yes, you shall have other company tomorrow night. The Lords of Kaldenstein shall give you a hearty welcome to their ancestral home."

A burst of mocking laughter died away in the distance as I fell to the floor in a dead faint.

## IV

I must have recovered somewhat after a time and dragged myself to the bed and again sunk into unconsciousness, for when I came around, daylight was streaming through the barred window of the room. I looked at my wristwatch. It was half-past three and, by the sun, it was afternoon, so the greater part of the day had passed.

I still felt weak, but struggled over to the window. It looked out upon the craggy slopes of the mountain, and there was no human habitation in sight. With a moan, I returned to the bed and tried to pray. I watched the patch of sunlight on the floor grow fainter and fainter until it had faded altogether. Then the shadows gathered and at last, only the dim outline of the window remained.

The darkness filled my soul with a new terror, and I lay on the bed in a cold, clammy sweat. Then I heard footsteps approaching, the door was flung open, and the Count entered bearing a candle.

"You must pardon me for what may seem shocking lack of manners on my part," he exclaimed, "but necessity compels me to keep to my chamber during the day. Now, however, I am able to offer you some entertainment."

I tried to rise, but my limbs refused to function. With a mirthless laugh he placed one arm around my waist and lifted me with as little effort as if I were a baby. In this fashion he carried me across the corridor and down the stairs into the hall.

Only three candles burned on the table, and I could see little of the room for some moments after he had dumped me into a chair. Then, as my eyes became accustomed to the gloom, I realized that there were two other guests at that board. The feeble light flickered on their faces, and I almost screamed with terror. I looked upon the ghastly countenances of dead men, every feature stamped with evil, and their eyes glowed with the same hellish light that shone in the Count's eyes.

"Allow me to introduce my uncle and my cousin," said my jailer. "August von Kaldenstein and Feodor von Kaldenstein."

"But," I blurted out, "I was told that Count Feodor died in 1645."

The three terrible creatures laughed heartily, as if I had recounted a good joke. Then August leaned over the table and pinched the fleshy part of my arm.

"He is full of good blood," he chuckled. "This feast has been long promised, Ludwig, but I think it has been worth waiting for."

I must have fainted at that, and when I came to myself I was lying on the table, and the three were bending over me. Their voices came in sibilant whispers.

"The throat must be mine," said the Count. "I claim the throat as my privilege."

"It should be mine," muttered August. "I am the eldest and it is long since I fed. Yet, I am content to have the breast."

"The legs are mine," croaked the third monster. "Legs are always full of rich, red blood."

Their lips were drawn back like the lips of animals, and their white fangs gleamed in the candlelight. Suddenly, a clanging sound disturbed the silence of the night. It was the castle bell. The creatures darted to the back of the dais and I could hear them muttering. Then the bell gave a more persistent peal.

"We are powerless against it," the Count cried. "Back to your retreat."

His two companions vanished through the small door which led to the underground chapel, and the Count of Kaldenstein stood alone in the center of the room. I raised myself into a sitting posture, and, as I did so, I heard a strong voice calling beyond the main door.

"Open in the Name of God," it thundered. "Open by the power of the ever Blessed Sacrament of the altar."

As if drawn by some overwhelming force, the Count approached the door and loosened the bolts. It was immediately flung open, and there stood the tall figure of the parish priest; bearing aloft something in a silver box like a watch. With him was the innkeeper, and I could see the poor fellow was terrified. The two advanced into the hall, and the Count retreated before them.

"Thrice in ten years have I frustrated you by the power of God," cried the priest. "Thrice has the Holy Sacrament been carried into this house of sin. Be warned in time, accursed man. Back to your foul tomb, creature of Satan. Back, I command you."

With a strange whimpering cry, the Count vanished through the small door, and the priest came over and assisted me from the table. The innkeeper produced a flask and forced some brandy between my lips, and I made an effort to stand.

"Foolish boy," said the priest. "You would not take my warning, and see what your folly has brought you to."

They helped me out of the castle and down the steps, but I collapsed before we reached the inn. I have a vague recollection of being helped into bed, and remember nothing more until I awakened in the morning.

The priest and the innkeeper were awaiting me in the dining room and we breakfasted together.

"What is the meaning of it all, Father?" I asked after the meal had been served.

"It is exactly as I told you," was the reply. "The Count of Kaldenstein is a vampire—he keeps the semblance of life in his evil body by drinking human blood. Eight years ago a headstrong youth, like yourself, determined to visit the castle. He did not return within reasonable time, and I had to save him from the clutches of the monster. Only by carrying with me the Body of Christ was I able to effect an entrance, and I was just in time. Then, two years later, a woman who professed to believe in neither God nor the Devil made up her mind to see the Count. Again, I was forced to bear the Blessed Sacrament into the castle, and, by its power, overcame the forces of Satan. Two days since I watched you climb the cliff and saw, with relief, that you returned safely. But yesterday morning, Heinrich came to inform me that your bed had not been slept in, and he was afraid the Count had got you. We waited until nightfall and then made our way up to the castle. The rest you know."

"I can never thank you both sufficiently for the manner in which you saved me from those creatures," I said.

"Creatures," repeated the priest in a surprised voice. "Surely there is only the Count? The servant does not share his master's blood-lust."

"No, I did not see the servant after he had admitted me. But there were two others—August and Feodor."

"August and Feodor," he murmured. "Then it is worse than we have ever dreamed. August died in 1572, and Feodor in 1645. Both were monsters of iniquity, but I did not suspect they were numbered among the living dead."

"Father," quavered the innkeeper. "We are not safe in our beds. Can we not call upon the government to rid us of these vampires?"

"The government would laugh at us," was the reply. "We must take the law into our own hands."

"What is to be done?" I asked.

"I wonder if you have the courage to see this ghastly

business through, and to witness a sight that will seem incredible?"

I assured him I was willing to do anything to help, for I considered I owed my life to him.

"Then," he said, "I will return to the church for a few things and we will go up to the castle. Will you come with us, Heinrich?"

The innkeeper hesitated just a moment, but it was evident that he had the greatest confidence in the priest, and he answered, "Of course I will, Father."

It was almost midday when we set off on our mysterious mission. The castle door stood wide open exactly as we had left it on the previous night, and the hall was deserted. We soon discovered the door under the tapestry, and the priest, with a powerful electric flashlight in his hand, led the way down the damp steps. At the chapel door, he paused and from his robes drew three crucifixes and a vessel of holy water. To each of us he handed one of the crosses, and sprinkled the door with the water. Then he opened it, and we entered the cavern.

With hardly a glance at the altar and its gruesome painting, he made his way to the entrance of the vault. It was locked, but he burst the catch with a powerful kick. A wave of fetid air leaped out at us and we staggered back. Then, lifting his crucifix before him and crying, "In the Name of the Father, the Son, and the Holy Ghost," the priest led us into the tomb. I do not know what I expected to see, but I gave a gasp of horror as the light revealed the interior of the place. In the center, resting on a wooden bier, was the sleeping body of the Count of Kaldenstein. His red lips were parted in a smile, and his wicked eyes were half open.

Around the vault, niches contained coffins, and the priest examined each in turn. Then he directed us to lift two of them to the floor. I noticed that one bore the name of August von Kaldenstein and the other that of Feodor. It took all our united strength to move the caskets, but at last we had them down. And all the time the eyes of the Count seemed to be watching us, although he never moved.

"Now," whispered the priest, "the most ghastly part of the business begins."

Producing a large screwdriver, he began to prise off the lid of the first coffin. Soon it was loose, and he motioned us to raise it. Inside was Count August looking exactly as I had seen him the previous night. His red-rimmed eyes were wide open and gleamed wickedly, and the stench of corruption hung about him. The priest set to work on the second casket, and soon revealed the body of Count Feodor, with his matted hair hanging about his white face.

Then began a strange ceremony. Taking the crucifixes from us, the priest laid them upon the breasts of the two bodies, and, producing his Breviary, recited some Latin prayers. Finally he stood back and flung holy water into the coffins. As the drops touched the leering corpses, they appeared to writhe in agony, to swell as though they were about to burst, and then, before our eyes, they crumbled into dust. Silently, we replaced the lids on the coffins and restored them to their niches.

"And now," said the priest, "we are powerless. Ludwig von Kaldenstein by evil arts has conquered death—for the time being at any rate—and we cannot treat him as we have treated these creatures whose vitality was only a semblance of life. We can but pray that God will curb the activities of this monster of sin."

So saying, he laid the third cross upon the Count's breast and, sprinkling him with holy water, uttered a Latin prayer. With that, we left the vault; but, as the door clanged behind us, something fell to the ground inside the place. It must have been the crucifix falling from the Count's breast.

We made our way up into the castle and never did God's good air taste sweeter. All this time, we had seen no sign of the old servant, and I suggested we should try to discover him. His quarters, I remembered, were in the north turret. There we found his crooked, old body hanging by the neck from a beam in the roof. He had been dead for at least twenty-four hours, and the priest said that nothing could be done other than to notify his death to the proper quarter and arrange for the funeral to take place.

I am still puzzled about the mystery of Kaldenstein Castle. The fact that Count August and Count Feodor had become vampires after death, although it sounds fantastic enough, is more easily understandable than Count Ludwig's seeming immunity from death. The priest could not explain the matter, and appeared to think that the Count might go on living and troubling the neighborhood for an indefinite period.

One thing I do know. On that last night at Kaldenstein, I opened my window before retiring to bed and looked out upon the castle. At the top of one of the turrets, clear in the bright moonlight, stood a black figure—the shadowy form of the Count of Kaldenstein.

Little more remains to be told. Of course, my stay in the village threw all my plans out, and by the time I arrived back at Munich my tour had taken nearly twenty days. Peter Schmidt laughed at me and wondered what blue-eyed maiden had caused me to linger in some Bavarian village. I didn't tell him that the real causes of the delay had been two dead men, and a third who, by all natural laws, should have been dead long ago.

# FREEZE-UP

*ANTHONY MASTERS*

MY PARENTS ARE GEOLOGISTS and we had come as a family to live and work at a base in the Antarctic. It was spring, and we were all amazed by the beauty of the place, with the ice breaking up into floes and gigantic bergs which shimmered a kaleidoscope of colors in the sunshine. They were an incredible sight on the deep, blue water, making a hollow booming sound as they majestically drifted south.

The base was sophisticated—a round metal building that had a micro-climate inside, a carefully controlled seventy degrees, which made the outside temperature, despite the sun, something of a shock. We even had a swimming pool in there, as well as a games room and a video lounge, so conditions weren't exactly what Captain Scott had to put up with.

But it certainly wasn't cushy. My parents were intrepid and we went for long journeys into the interior, studying rock formations emerging from the glaciers. Because I was taking a term off school, I had to do some studying—but as I wanted to be a geologist, I was finding our work in the Antarctic fascinating. Until that awful day.

"Here's a big berg coming up, Matt."

I can still see us now. My mother and I were standing by the shore, taking turns staring out into the sound through her binoculars while Dad checked over some equipment in the base. As usual, we were surrounded by raucous penguins, and the stink of guano, their droppings, was enhanced by the onshore wind.

The berg had drifted into the bay, right up to the slowly melting ice floes. It was as tall as a four-story building, and had the most incredible electric-blue sheen to its gleaming, translucent surface.

"Wait a minute." Mom handed me the binoculars, her voice shaking with excitement. "There's something in that ice."

I soon saw what she was on about. Frozen into the ice was a giant wolf.

"It's enormous," I whispered.

My mother nodded. "And old."

"Old?"

"Could be neolithic," she said hopefully. "The wolf might have been in the ice for centuries. This is a real find."

"What are we going to do?" I asked, wondering if my mother was getting carried away.

The berg was drifting nearer now in the strong breeze, and as I stared at it through the binoculars, I could see that the eyes of the giant wolf were open; for a moment I had the foolish but uncomfortable feeling that it was watching us.

"This onshore wind should keep the berg here for a few more hours of daylight, but we need cutting equipment first. We'll get the wolf out and put it in one of the deep freezers. Then we'll take a look at it in the lab. Of course, it's going to be the biologists' baby," Mom said regretfully. "Anyway, he makes a change from inanimate rocks."

"How do you know the wolf's a 'he'?" I asked, amused by all the assumptions my mother was making. She seemed to have completely abandoned her usual procedure of scientific reasoning.

"I've got a hunch," Mom replied.

*

Her hunch proved to be correct. The wolf *was* a male, and when cut out of the glistening ice, he was much larger than I had imagined and perfectly preserved.

"It must have gotten trapped in the ice," said Professor Lomas, the chief biologist on the base, as all the scientists gathered around the table in the lab on which the beast lay.

The hide of the wolf was jet black, and his enormous limbs, spread out on the table, looked as powerful as they must have been when he was alive. In fact it was hard to believe the thing was really dead.

"What happens if he gets properly thawed out?" I asked the professor.

"He'll disintegrate, so he's going back on ice. What a specimen. Who would have thought the beast could have remained intact for centuries like this?"

"Were wolves all as big as he is then?" I asked.

The professor shook his head. "He's special."

That night, just before I went to bed, I met Professor Lomas in the corridor.

"I'm going to put the wolf back on the table," he told me. "I want to take another look."

"Why?" I asked.

But the professor didn't reply. Instead he said, "Would you be prepared to give me a hand lifting him out of the freezer? I was going to wake one of the lab assistants but they're both on early shift and—"

"Of course I'll help," I replied.

In the end we only just managed to lift the wolf from the freezer to the table. At one point we staggered, and for a moment I thought we were going to drop him on the floor. I also had the strangest feeling that for a split second the thing had moved. But the wolf was frozen solid and had been dead for centuries, and I dismissed the idea as ridiculous, born out of my own fatigue.

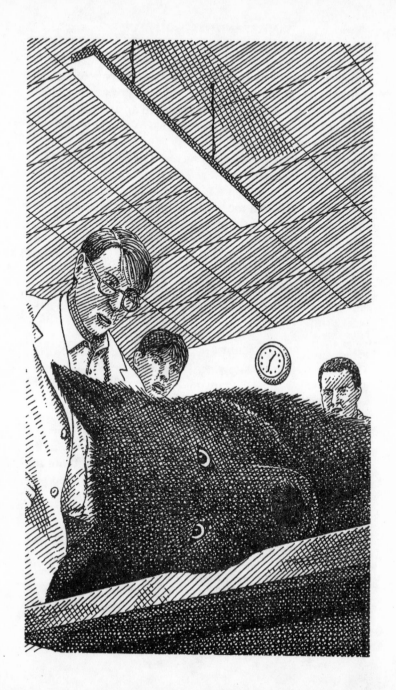

"That'll do," snapped Professor Lomas abruptly, and when I met his gaze I saw that he was looking impatient, as if he wanted to be alone with the wolf and resented every moment of my presence. Reluctantly, he managed an apologetic smile. "Thank you, but I have further studies to complete and they may take me some time."

I wanted to ask what they were, but took the hint and went to bed. It was some time before I slept.

I woke early the next morning, well before my parents were up. The lab was not far from my bedroom so I decided to take a stroll over there, although I was far from certain whether I was going to get a good reception. If Professor Lomas was still there, it wouldn't be the first time he'd worked all night. He was a man consumed by his work and I had often almost envied him for that. To have such burning curiosity must be wonderful.

When I reached the lab, I saw that the door was half-open. This surprised me, knowing Professor Lomas's obsession with privacy. I paused, knowing how angry he would be if I just barged in. Hesitantly, I crept toward the half-open door so that I could just peer around it and then quickly back off before he saw me. Curiously, the room appeared to be empty. The table was bare, so he had clearly put the wolf back in the freezer, although how he had managed to do so without my help I couldn't imagine. Maybe he had had to resort to waking up one of the lab assistants.

Then I saw the red lake on the floor.

Professor Lomas was lying on his back, his eyes open and staring ahead, his lips twisted in a snarl of surprised, frenzied horror. There were teeth marks on his neck and face. The blood was everywhere.

I went to the freezer and opened it. The space was empty. I wheeled around, expecting to see the huge wolf crouched in a corner, waiting for me, but there was no sign of the beast.

54

My gaze returned to what had been Professor Lomas, and I stared down into his sightless eyes while my mind raced in circles, returning again and again to the conclusion that I didn't want to accept: the wolf had somehow become animated and the little movement I had felt had been the first stirrings of renewed life. Now the thing was free and prowling the base, searching for more victims.

Somehow, I forced myself outside the lab and raced down the corridor to my parents' bedroom, thinking the wolf would leap out on me at any moment. But I reached them in safety and slammed the door shut behind me with relief. It took some time to convince them of what had happened to Professor Lomas.

"I'll go and check," said my father at last. "You're in shock, Matt, and . . ."

He went to the door in his bathrobe but I yelled at him in panic, "Don't go outside, Dad. For God's sake—don't go outside."

"Sit down."

But by this time, I was barring the door. "Don't you see—it's wandering the base. You haven't seen—what it did to him."

My father went to a cupboard and took out a handgun. "Emergency use only," he muttered and tried to smile reassuringly.

I stood aside reluctantly as he walked out into the soft light of the corridor.

The wail of the emergency siren went off just as my father returned, looking shocked and ill. "*Something* got him," he muttered. "It's unbelievable."

"The wolf—" I began.

"How can a creature like that, frozen in ice for centuries, reanimate? It's just a coincidence the carcass has disappeared. Someone must be—"

"I felt it coming back to life, Dad. Don't you see—we've released it."

55

"There's no sign of the thing," he snapped. "Someone attacked Lomas and took the wolf. Professional jealousy can be—"

"Leaving teeth marks on him like that? It's out there somewhere," I promised him.

The wail of the siren was cut short by an announcement over the Tannoy. "Attention. Attention. We are on Red Alert. Repeat. We are on Red Alert. It is essential that all personnel remain in their quarters. We have a large animal loose on the base. The animal has been located and is about to be shot. Keep your doors closed. I repeat. Keep your doors closed until you are notified that the Red Alert is over." The voice was replaced by the renewed wail of the siren.

The knocking on our door was panic-stricken and my mother rushed to open it. Ted Morgan, one of the security men, flung himself in and slammed the door. He acted only just in time, for seconds later it shuddered with an enormous impact. But the door held, although the impact came again and again.

Then there was a long silence while Morgan, my parents, and I watched the door in terror, waiting for another attack, waiting for it to splinter, wondering if, with a terrible sound of rending wood, the thing would be upon us.

Still shaking, Morgan sank down on the bed. "Bob," he muttered over and over again. "Bob."

"He's dead?"

"It ripped him to pieces. There was nothing I could do for him. Nothing."

"But you were both armed," said my father unbelievingly. "Why didn't you shoot the wolf?"

"I did," said Ted Morgan. "I emptied this gun into it. But the bullets didn't have the slightest effect."

"It *must* be badly wounded," I said hopefully.

"There wasn't a mark on him," replied Morgan.

Something stirred in my mind. A legend. An impossible legend.

"Suppose it was all true," I blurted out. "Not a myth after all."

"True?" Morgan turned on me in angry frustration. "What the hell are you on about?"

"You don't understand," I said impatiently. "I mean we could be dealing with a werewolf."

They all three stared at me in amazement, and although a look of angry contempt immediately crossed Morgan's face, my parents remained uneasily silent.

"This isn't time for jokes," Ted Morgan said angrily.

"It's *not* a joke," I insisted, suddenly confident that I was right. "I mean it. And you'll only destroy that wolf with silver bullets."

Morgan laughed contemptuously. "And how do you come to that conclusion?"

"I read it in a graphic novel—kind of comic book," I added unguardedly.

He laughed again, harshly sarcastic.

"Wait a minute," said my mother. "It's also recorded in folklore. I remember reading it as a child."

"If real bullets don't work," said my father, "why not *try* silver? What have we got to lose?"

"Because we don't just have them lying around." Ted Morgan was incredulous now, gazing at all three of us as if we were completely crazy.

"Silver bullets could be made easily in the lab," said my mother. "All we need to do is melt down part of the director's tea service and use an ordinary bullet as a measure. It could take—an hour or so."

"While that thing's on the rampage?" Morgan wasn't convinced; he just seemed stunned at the sheer lunacy of the idea.

"Anything's worth a try," said my mother.

The thundering on our door began again, but this time it was the desperate beating of human fists. Morgan opened the door a crack and John Slater, the director, pushed his way in.

"The damn thing's devouring somebody in the gym. God knows how I got past it. There was nothing I could do for the—"

My father interrupted, not wanting Slater to go on for our sake or his. "Is it—still eating?"

"Yes."

"I'm going to the laboratory on my own." He looked meaningfully at my mother. "Three of us can't risk being attacked."

Reluctantly, she agreed.

"I'm going with you," I insisted.

But he was adamant. "No one's going with me. No one at all. Stay here—I'll be back as soon as I can." He took Ted Morgan's gun, opened the door, peered outside, and then vanished up the empty corridor.

Time passed with aching slowness, and the tension between us all reached such a pitch that I found it increasingly difficult to breathe. I repeatedly looked at my watch, praying for my father, trying to blot out all thought of the deadly creature outside. But I failed, seeing the werewolf at the door of the lab with my dad working desperately against the clock inside. I saw the thing run at the door—I saw the door splintering, buckling under its weight. Then I saw the wolf landing on his shoulders, bearing him down to the floor while its teeth . . . Again, yet again, I stared helplessly down at the relentless hands of my watch and saw that, somehow, an hour had passed.

"I'm going after him," said Morgan. "I can't take this any longer."

"That would be very foolish." Slater stood with his back to the door, but Morgan was determined.

"Get out of my way!"

"I *order* you not to go." Slater still stood there, while my mother and I felt the tension in the room increase to unbearable heights.

Morgan ignored him and pushed straight past him. "Bolt this up tight and don't try to follow me," he said as he wrenched open the door.

*

The werewolf sprang, its huge teeth buried in Morgan's throat, while my mother and I watched helplessly.

With a sinking heart I realized that the werewolf would simply gorge itself on us all, one by one.

My father stood on the threshold, his face twisted in loathing, gripping Ted Morgan's gun and aiming it at the wolf. But he had arrived too late for the security guard.

A wave of helplessness swept over me as he aimed the gun at the werewolf's head. His hand was shaking as the creature looked up at him, but I saw—or thought I saw—a knowledge in the wolf's eyes.

He fired again and again, the silver bullets penetrating the head and then the body. There were little soft splats as they made contact, but there was no blood, no tissue. The thing swayed, feebly sprang at my father—and swayed again. Then the wolf fell on its side, splayed right across the center of the small room, thrashed wildly and at last lay still.

"It's dissolving," said Slater unbelievingly. He was wrong. A haze of steam rose, and we saw that the fur and sinew were undergoing a change. A few minutes later, the steamlike substance cleared and to our amazement we could see a large man, completely naked, with an apelike forehead.

"He's neolithic," breathed Slater, but in seconds the body began to decompose before our eyes. Soon there was nothing more than a pool of dark, stagnant water on the carpet.

# DRINK MY BLOOD

## RICHARD MATHESON

THE PEOPLE ON THE BLOCK decided definitely that Jules was crazy when they heard about his composition. There had been suspicions for a long time. He made people shiver with his blank stare. His coarse, guttural tongue sounded unnatural in his frail body. The paleness of his skin upset many children. It seemed to hang loose around his flesh. He hated sunlight.

And, his ideas were a little out of place for the people who lived on the block.

Jules wanted to be a vampire.

People declared it common knowledge that he was born on a night when winds uprooted trees. They said he was born with three teeth. They said he'd used them to fasten himself on his mother's breast, drawing blood with the milk.

They said he used to cackle and bark in his crib after dark. They said he walked at two months and sat staring at the moon whenever it shone.

Those were things that people said.

His parents were always worried about him. An only child, they noticed his flaws quickly.

They thought he was blind until the doctor told them it was

60

just a vacuous stare. He told them that Jules, with his large head, might be a genius or an idiot. It turned out he was an idiot.

He never spoke a word until he was five. Then one night coming up to supper, he sat down at the table and said, "Death."

His parents were torn between delight and disgust. They finally settled for a place in-between the two feelings. They decided that Jules couldn't have realized what the word meant.

But Jules did.

From that night on, he built up such a large vocabulary that everyone who knew him was astonished. He not only acquired every word spoken to him, words from signs, magazines, books; he made up his own words.

Like, nighttouch. Or, killove. They were really several words that melted into each other. They said things Jules felt but couldn't explain with other words.

He used to sit on the porch while the other children played hopscotch, stickball, and other games. He sat there and stared at the sidewalk, and made up words.

Until he was twelve, Jules kept pretty much out of trouble. Of course, there was the time they found him undressing Olive Jones in an alley. And another time he was discovered dissecting a kitten on his bed.

But there were many years in-between. Those scandals were forgotten.

In general, he went through childhood merely disgusting people.

He went to school, but never studied. He spent about two or three years in each grade. The teachers all knew him by his first name. In some subjects, like reading and writing, he was almost brilliant.

In others, he was hopeless.

One Saturday when he was twelve, Jules went to the movies. He saw *Dracula*.

When the show was over he walked, a throbbing nerve mass, through the little-girl and -boy ranks.

He went home and locked himself in the bathroom for two hours.

His parents pounded on the door and threatened but he wouldn't come out.

Finally, he unlocked the door and sat down at the supper table. He had a bandage on his thumb and a satisfied look on his face.

The morning after, he went to the library. It was Sunday. He sat on the steps all day, waiting for it to open. Finally he went home.

The next day he came back instead of going to school.

He found *Dracula* on the shelves. He couldn't borrow it because he wasn't a member and to be a member, he had to bring in one of his parents.

So he stuck the book down his pants and left the library and never brought it back.

He went to the park and sat down and read the book through. It was late evening before he finished.

He started at the beginning again, reading as he ran from streetlight to streetlight, all the way home.

He didn't hear a word of the scolding he got for missing lunch and supper. He ate, went in his room, and read the book to the finish. They asked him where he got the book. He said he found it.

As the days passed, Jules read the story over and over. He never went to school.

Late at night, when he had fallen into an exhausted slumber, his mother used to take the book into the living room and show it to her husband.

One night they noticed that Jules had underlined certain sentences with dark, shaky, pencil lines.

Like: "The lips were crimson with fresh blood and the stream had trickled over her chin and stained the purity of her lawn death-robe."

Or: "When the blood began to spurt out, he took my hands in one of his, holding them tight and, with the other seized my neck and pressed my mouth to the wound . . . ."

When his mother saw this, she threw the book down the garbage chute.

The next morning when Jules found the book missing he screamed and twisted his mother's arm until she told him where the book was.

Then he ran down to the basement and dug in the piles of garbage until he found the book.

Coffee grounds and egg yolk on his hands and wrists, he went to the park and read it again.

For a month, he read the book avidly. Then he knew it so well he threw it away and just thought about it.

Absence notes were coming from school. His mother yelled. Jules decided to go back for a while.

He wanted to write a composition.

One day he wrote it in class. When everyone was finished writing, the teacher asked if anyone wanted to read their composition to the class.

Jules raised his hand.

The teacher was surprised. But she felt charity. She wanted to encourage him. She drew in her tiny jab of a chin and smiled.

"Alright," she said, "pay attention, children. Jules is going to read us his composition."

Jules stood up. He was excited. The paper shook in his hands.

"My Ambition, by . . ."

"Come to the front of the class, Jules, dear."

Jules went to the front of the class. The teacher smiled lovingly. Jules started again.

"My Ambition, by Jules Dracula."

The smile sagged.

"When I grow up, I want to be a vampire."

The teacher's smiling lips jerked down and out. Her eyes popped wide.

"I want to live forever and get even with everybody and make all the girls vampires. I want to smell of death."

"Jules!"

"I want to have a foul breath that stinks of dead earth and crypts and sweet coffins."

63

The teacher shuddered. Her hands twitched on her green blotter. She couldn't believe her ears. She looked at the children. They were gaping. Some of them were giggling. But not the girls.

"I want to be all cold and have rotten flesh with stolen blood in the veins."

"That will . . . hrrumph!"

The teacher cleared her throat mightily.

"That will be all, Jules," she said.

Jules talked louder and desperately.

"I want to sink my terrible white teeth in my victims' necks. I want them to . . ."

"Jules! Go to your seat this instant!"

"I want them to slide like razors in the flesh and into the veins," read Jules ferociously.

The teacher jolted to her feet. Children were shivering. None of them were giggling.

"Then I want to draw my teeth out and let the blood flow easy in my mouth and run hot in my throat and . . ."

The teacher grabbed his arm. Jules tore away and ran to a corner. Barricaded behind a stool, he yelled:

"And drip off my tongue and run out of my lips down my victims' throats! I want to drink girls' blood!"

The teacher lunged for him. She dragged him out of the corner. He clawed at her and screamed all the way to the door and the principal's office.

"That is my ambition! That is my ambition! That is my ambition!"

It was grim.

Jules was locked in his room. The teacher and the principal sat with Jules' parents. They were talking in sepulchral voices.

They were recounting the scene.

All along the block, parents were discussing it. Most of them didn't believe it at first. They thought their children made it up.

Then they thought what horrible children they'd raised if the children could make up such things.

So they believed it.

After that, everyone watched Jules like a hawk. People avoided his touch and look. Parents pulled their children off the street when he approached. Everyone whispered tales of him.

There were more absence notes.

Jules told his mother he wasn't going to school any more. Nothing would change his mind. He never went again.

When an attendance officer came to the apartment, Jules would run over the roofs until he was far away from there.

A year wasted by.

Jules wandered the streets searching for something; he didn't know what. He looked in alleys. He looked in garbage cans. He looked in lots. He looked on the east side and the west side and in the middle.

He couldn't find what he wanted.

He rarely slept. He never spoke. He stared down all the time. He forgot his special words.

Then.

One day in the park, Jules strolled through the zoo.

An electric shock passed through him when he saw the vampire bat.

His eyes grew wide and his discolored teeth shone dully in a wide smile.

From that day on, Jules went daily to the zoo and looked at the bat. He spoke to it and called it the Count. He felt in his heart it was really a man who had changed.

A rebirth of culture struck him.

He stole another book from the library. It told all about wildlife.

He found the page on the vampire bat. He tore it out and threw the book away.

He learned the section by heart.

He knew how the bat made its wound. How it lapped up the blood like a kitten drinking cream. How it walked on folded wing stalks and hind legs like a black furry spider. Why it took no nourishment but blood.

Month after month, Jules stared at the bat and talked to it. It became the one comfort in his life. The one symbol of dreams come true.

*

One day Jules noticed that the bottom of the wire covering the cage had become loose.

He looked around, his black eyes shifting. He didn't see anyone looking. It was a cloudy day. Not many people were there.

Jules tugged at the wire.

It moved a little.

Then he saw a man come out of the monkey house. So he pulled back his hand and strolled away, whistling a song he had just made up.

Late at night, when he was supposed to be asleep, he would walk barefoot past his parents' room. He would hear his father and mother snoring. He would hurry out, put on his shoes, and run to the zoo.

Every time the watchman was not around, Jules would tug at the wiring.

He kept on pulling it loose.

When he had finished and had to run home, he pushed the wire in again. Then no one could tell.

All day Jules would stand in front of the cage and look at the Count and chuckle and tell him he'd soon be free again.

He told the Count all the things he knew. He told the Count he was going to practice climbing down walls headfirst.

He told the Count not to worry. He'd soon be out. Then, together, they could go all around and drink girls' blood.

One night Jules pulled the wire out and crawled under it into the cage.

It was very dark.

He crept on his knees to the little wooden house. He listened to see if he could hear the Count squeaking.

He stuck his arm in the black doorway. He kept whispering.

He jumped when he felt a needle jab in his finger.

With a look of great pleasure on his thin face, Jules drew the fluttering hairy bat to him.

He climbed down from the cage with it and ran out of the zoo; out of the park. He ran down the silent streets.

It was getting late in the morning. Light touched the dark skies with gray. He couldn't go home. He had to have a place.

He went down an alley and climbed over a fence. He held tight to the bat. It lapped at the dribble of blood from his finger.

He went across a yard and into a little deserted shack.

It was dark inside and damp. It was full of rubble and tin cans and soggy cardboard and excrement.

Jules made sure there was no way the bat could escape.

Then he pulled the door tight and put a stick through the metal loop.

He felt his heart beating hard and his limbs trembling.

He let go of the bat. It flew to a dark corner and hung on the wood.

Jules feverishly tore off his shirt. His lips shook. He smiled a crazy smile.

He reached down into his pants' pocket and took out a little pocketknife he had stolen from his mother.

He opened it and ran a finger over the blade. It sliced through the flesh.

With shaking fingers he jabbed at his throat. He hacked. The blood ran through his fingers.

"Count! Count!" he cried in frenzied joy. "Drink my red blood! Drink me! Drink me!"

He stumbled over the tin cans and slipped and felt for the bat. It sprang from the wood and soared across the shack and fastened itself on the outer side.

Tears ran down Jules' cheeks.

He gritted his teeth. The blood ran across his shoulders and across his thin, hairless chest.

His body shook in fever. He staggered back toward the other side. He tripped and felt his side torn open on the sharp edge of a tin can.

His hands went out. They clutched the bat. He placed it against his throat. He sank on his back on the cool wet earth. He sighed.

He started to moan and clutch at his chest. His stomach heaved. The black bat on his neck silently lapped his blood.

Jules felt his life seeping away.

He thought of all the years past. The waiting. His parents. School. Dracula. Dreams. For this. This sudden glory.

Jules' eyes flickered open.

The side of the reeking shack swam around him.

It was hard to breathe. He opened his mouth to gasp in the air. He sucked it in. It was foul. It made him cough. His skinny body lurched on the cold ground.

Mists crept away in his brain.

One by one like drawn veils.

Suddenly his mind was filled with terrible clarity.

He knew he was lying half-naked on garbage and letting a flying bat drink his blood.

With a strangled cry, he reached up and tore away the furry throbbing bat. He flung it away from him. It came back, fanning his face with its vibrating wings.

Jules staggered to his feet.

He felt for the door. He could hardly see. He tried to stop his throat from bleeding so.

He managed to get the door open.

Then, lurching into the dark yard, he fell on his face in the long grass blades.

He tried to call out for help.

But no sounds, save a bubbling mockery of words, came from his lips.

He heard the fluttering wings.

Then, suddenly, they were gone.

Strong fingers lifted him gently. Through dying eyes, Jules saw a tall, dark, man whose eyes shone like rubies.

"My son," the man said.

# DAYBLOOD

*ROGER ZELAZNY*

I CROUCHED IN THE CORNER of the collapsed shed behind the ruined church. The dampness soaked through the knees of my jeans, but I knew that my wait was just about ended. Picturesquely, a few tendrils of mist rose from the soaked ground, to be stirred feebly by predawn breezes. How Hollywood of the weather . . . .

I cast my gaze around the lightening sky, guessing correctly as to the direction of arrival. Within a minute I saw them flapping their way back—a big, dark one and a smaller, pale one. Predictably, they entered the church through the opening where a section of the roof had years before fallen in. I suppressed a yawn as I checked my watch. Fifteen minutes from now they should be settled and dozing as the sun spills morning all over the east. Possibly a little sooner, but give them a bit of leeway. No hurry yet.

I stretched and cracked my knuckles. I'd rather be home in bed. Nights are for sleeping, not for playing nursemaid to a couple of stupid vampires.

Yes, Virginia, there really are vampires. Nothing to get excited about, though. Odds are you'll never meet one. There just aren't that many around. In fact, they're damn near an endangered

70

species—which is entirely understandable, considering the general level of intelligence I've encountered among them.

Take this guy Brodsky as an example. He lives—pardon me, resides—near a town containing several thousand people. He could have visited a different person each night without ever repeating himself, leaving his caterers (I understand that's their in-term these days) with little more than a slight sore throat, a touch of temporary anaemia and a couple of soon-to-be-forgotten scratches on the neck.

But no. He took a fancy to a local beauty—one Elaine Wilson, ex-majorette. Kept going back for more. Pretty soon she entered the customary coma and underwent the *nosferatu* transformation. All right, I know I said there aren't that many of them around—and personally I do feel that the world could use a few more vampires. But it's not a population-pressure thing with Brodsky, just stupidity and greed. No real finesse, no planning. While I applaud the creation of another member of the Un-Dead, I am sufficiently appalled by the carelessness of his methods to consider serious action. He left a trail that just about anybody could trace here; he also managed to display so many of the traditional signs and leave such a multitude of clues that even in these modern times a reasonable person could become convinced of what was going on.

Poor old Brodsky—still living in the Middle Ages and behaving just as he did in the days of their population boom. It apparently never occurred to him to consider the mathematics of that sort of thing. He drains a few people he becomes particularly attracted to and they become *nosferatu*. If they feel and behave the same way they go out and recruit a few more of their caterers. And so on. It's like a chain letter. After a time, everyone would be *nosferatu* and there wouldn't be any caterers left. Then what? Fortunately, nature has ways of dealing with population explosions, even at this level. Still, a sudden rash of recruits in this mass-media age could really mess up the underground ecosystem.

So much for philosophy. Time to get inside and beat the crowd.

I picked up my plastic bag and worked my way out of the shed, cursing softly when I bumped against a post and brought a shower down over me. I made my way through the field then, and up to the side door of the old building. It was secured by a rusty padlock which I snapped and threw into the distant cemetery.

Inside, I perched myself on the sagging railing of the choir section and opened my bag. I withdrew my sketchbook and the pencil I'd brought along. Light leaked in through the broken window to the rear. What it fell upon was mostly trash. Not a particularly inspiring scene. Whatever . . . I began sketching it. It's always good to have a hobby that can serve as an excuse for odd actions, as an ice-breaker . . . .

Ten minutes, I guessed. At most.

Six minutes later, I heard their voices. They weren't particularly noisy, but I have exceptionally acute hearing. There were three of them, as I'd guessed there would be.

They entered through the side door also, slinking, jumpy—looking all around and seeing nothing. At first they didn't even notice me creating art where childish voices had filled Sunday mornings with off-key praise in years gone by.

There was old Dr. Morgan, several wooden stakes protruding from his black bag (I'll bet there was a hammer in there, too—I guess the Hippocratic Oath doesn't extend to the Un-Dead—*primum, non nocere*, etc.); and Father O'Brien, clutching his Bible like a shield, crucifix in his other hand; and young Ben Kelman (Elaine's fiancé), with a shovel over his shoulder and a bag from which I suspected the sudden odor of garlic to have it's origin.

I cleared my throat and all three of them stopped, turned, bumped into each other.

"Hi, Doc," I said. "Hi, Father. Ben . . . ."

"Wayne!" Doc said. "What are you doing here?"

"Sketching," I said. "I'm into old buildings these days."

"The hell you are!" Ben said. "Excuse me, Father . . . You're just after a story for your damned newspaper!"

I shook my head.

"Really I'm not."

"Well, Gus'd never let you print anything about this and you know it."

"Honest," I said. "I'm not here for a story. But I know why you're here, and you're right—even if I wrote it up it would never appear. You really believe in vampires?"

Doc fixed me with a steady gaze.

"Not until recently," he said. "But son, if you'd seen what we've seen, you'd believe."

I nodded my head and closed my sketchpad.

"All right," I replied, "I'll tell you. I'm here because I'm curious. I wanted to see it for myself, but I don't want to go down there alone. Take me with you."

They exchanged glances.

"I don't know . . ." Ben said.

"It won't be anything for the squeamish," Doc told me.

Father O'Brien just nodded.

"I don't know about having anyone else in on this," Ben added.

"How many more know about it?" I asked.

"It's just us, really," Ben explained. "We're the only ones who actually saw him in action."

"A good newspaperman knows when to keep his mouth shut," I said, "but he's also a very curious creature. Let me come along."

Ben shrugged and Doc nodded. After a moment Father O'Brien nodded too.

I replaced my pad and pencil in the bag and got down from the railing.

I followed them across the church, out into a short hallway and up into an open, sagging door. Doc flicked on a flashlight and played it upon a rickety flight of stairs leading down into darkness. Slowly then, he began to descend. Father O'Brien followed him. The stairs groaned and seemed to move. Ben and I waited till they had reached the bottom. Then Ben stuffed his bag of pungent groceries inside his jacket and withdrew a flashlight from his pocket. He turned it on and stepped down. I was right behind him.

I halted when we reached the foot of the stair. In the beams from their lights I beheld the two caskets set up on sawhorses, also the thing on the wall above the larger one.

"Father, what is that?" I pointed.

Someone obligingly played a beam of light upon it.

"It looks like a sprig of mistletoe tied to the figure of a little stone deer," he said.

"Probably has something to do with black magic," I offered.

He crossed himself, went over to it and removed it.

"Probably so," he said, crushing the mistletoe and throwing it across the room, shattering the figure on the floor and kicking the pieces away.

I smiled, I moved forward then.

"Let's get things open and have a look," Doc said.

I lent them a hand.

When the caskets were open I ignored the comments about paleness, preservation, and bloody mouths. Brodsky looked the same as he always did—dark hair, heavy dark eyebrows, sagging jowls, a bit of a paunch. The girl was lovely, though. Taller than I'd thought, however, with a very faint pulsation at the throat and an almost bluish cast to her skin.

Father O'Brien opened his Bible and began reading, holding the flashlight above it with a trembling hand. Doc placed his bag upon the floor and fumbled around inside it.

Ben turned away, tears in his eyes. I reached out then and broke his neck quietly while the others were occupied. I lowered him to the floor and stepped up beside Doc.

"What—?" he began, and that was his last word.

Father O'Brien stopped reading. He stared at me across his Bible.

"You work for *them*?" he said hoarsely, darting a glance at the caskets.

"Hardly," I said, "but I need them. They're my life's blood."

"I don't understand . . . ."

"Everything is prey to something else, and we do what we must. That's ecology. Sorry, Father."

74

I used Ben's shovel to bury the three of them beneath an earthen section of the floor toward the rear—garlic, stakes, and all. Then I closed the caskets and carried them up the stairs.

I checked around as I hiked across a field and back up the road after the pickup truck. It was still relatively early and there was no one around.

I loaded them both in back and covered them with a tarp. It was a thirty-mile drive to another ruined church I knew of.

Later, when I had installed them safely in their new quarters, I penned a note and placed it in Brodsky's hand:

> Dear B,
>
> Let this be a lesson to you. You are going to have to stop acting like Bela Lugosi. You lack his class. You are lucky to be waking up at all this night. In the future be more circumspect in your activities or I may retire you myself. After all, I'm not here to serve you.
>
> Yours truly,
>
> W
>
> P.S. The mistletoe and the statue of Cernunnos don't work anymore. Why did you suddenly get superstitious?

I glanced at my watch as I left the place. It was eleven-fifteen. I stopped at a 7-11 a little later and used their outside phone.

"Hi Kiela," I said when I heard her voice. "It's me."

"Werdeth," she said. "It's been a while."

"I know. I've been busy."

"With what?"

"Do you know where the old Church of the Apostles out off Route 6 is?"

"Of course. It's on my backup list, too."

"Meet me there at twelve thirty and I'll tell you about it over lunch."

# TERROR IN THE TATRAS

*WINIFRED FINLAY*

O N THE OUTSKIRTS of a village in the foothills of the Tatra Mountains in Poland, there once dwelt a forester and his wife, with two children, a girl and a boy, whom they loved dearly.

When summer came, the children played in front of the two-roomed, wooden cottage the forester himself had built, and his wife spun and wove and sewed, while her husband worked in the pine forests that stretched up the great mountain ranges to the east and to the north.

But all too soon, the winter was on them, when the days were dark, the winds bitter, and the snow came whirling down, covering cottages and ground and trees.

First the pond and then the river froze, and, as it grew steadily colder and colder and the snow continued to fall, from high up in the forests came the first howls of foraging wolf packs. Then, all the work out-of-doors had to be done in the short hours of daylight, and the forester and other men of the village were careful never to venture far into the forest alone, and they always returned home before nightfall and saw all doors were barred, all windows firmly closed.

As the cold increased, the howls of the hungry wolves grew

louder as they searched for food, for an unwary hare or fox, for a reindeer weakened by injury, or a bear grown too old to defend itself; but sometimes, when the hunt had been unsuccessful and the villagers looked out of their windows in the pale light of the early morning, they saw the dreaded prints in the fallen snow and they hurried out to make sure their pigs and geese and ducks and hens were safe in the outhouses and cellars.

Each year the long cruel winter claimed its victims, generally from among the very old or the very young.

It was early one spring, when the girl was nine and her brother seven, that their mother took to her bed and died.

"What is to become of us now?" the forester asked despairingly when they returned to the cottage after the funeral.

"I have already put some of our bread and goat's-milk cheese in your bag," the little girl said. "Take your ax and go into the forest and work as you have always done. My brother and I will look after you and our home and all our stock."

Shaking his head doubtfully, the forester did as he was bid. Heavy-hearted, he worked in the forest and, heavy-hearted, he returned home, but the minute he opened the door and saw the floor swept, the beds made, and the dumplings bobbing around in the soup in the iron caldron above the fire, he gathered the children in his arms and wept for the last time.

"I shall miss your mother for the rest of my life," he said, "but together we shall look after one another."

"Will the pain inside of me always hurt?" the little boy asked that night.

"It will grow less until you scarcely feel it," his sister assured him, and she hoped that this would indeed be so.

As the summer months passed the children still missed their mother, but because they worked so hard in the cottage and in the common fields which belonged to everyone in the village, their grief, although they did not realize it, was not quite as sharp as it had been.

They prepared for the winter exactly as their mother had

done, drying herbs and plants, berries and mushrooms, and fungi, and salting their share of the birds and beasts for which the villagers had decided there would not be enough food and so had slaughtered and divided among the households.

The last carp were caught in the village pond, the last trout in the river before they were frozen over, and once again the bitter winds flew down from the north bringing with them the swirling snowflakes, and it was not long before the hungry wolves ventured nearer and nearer the village by night in search of something—anything—to eat.

One evening, the forester returned late from a meeting the priest had called to arrange for a fatherless family to be cared for: the children were asleep on their straw mattresses in front of the kitchen fire and, pausing only to adjust the woven blankets and the sheepskins which covered them, he went quietly to his lonely bed in the other room and quickly fell asleep.

Presently he stirred uneasily and then sat up, wondering why it was so light and then realizing that although he had double-barred the door, he had forgotten to close the shutters of his little window, and the moon had risen, and was peering in with its pale, unearthly light.

Drawing around him the fur pelts which his wife had sewn together as their bed covering, he stared, fascinated by the dazzling circle of light, wondering why he had never before noticed how big and splendid, and at the same time how frightening, the moon was. He leaned forward to look more closely, but suddenly the rays were cut off as the head of an animal covered with white fur and with deep-set eyes appeared at the window, and first one paw was raised, and then a second, as though in entreaty. When the animal saw that it held his attention, it threw back its head so that the moonlight caught its strange dark eyes as it howled, mournfully, but very softly.

"A wolf!" he cried in horror. He leaped out of bed, pulled on his clothes and boots, and seizing his lantern and gun, walked quickly and quietly through the kitchen. But as he drew back the second of the heavy wooden bars which held the door securely closed, his daughter stirred.

"What is it, Father?" she asked sleepily.

"A wolf. A great white wolf. I mean to go out and shoot it. Bar the door after me, child."

"Oh, Father, it is not safe for you to go out alone at night," the little girl cried, but the snowflakes swirling in the moonlight dazzled her, and though she could hear her father shouting at the creature, and caught occasional glimpses of his lantern as he entered the forest, it seemed to her that all the world outside was filled with the eerie howling of the wolf, and as it grew fainter and fainter, she thought she could distinguish a mocking note such as she had never heard before in the cry of any wild animal.

Troubled, she barred the door, hesitated and then opened the shutters of the kitchen window so that the firelight might shine out, and returned to her bed.

And waited.

Farther and farther into the woods the forester plunged, where frozen snow weighed down the branches of the pine trees: on and on he forced his way, following the tracks of the great white wolf until the moonlight no longer penetrated the snow-shrouded canopy of interlocking branches, and he was completely dependent on his lantern.

What a magnificent creature it was. And white! It was the first time he had ever seen a white wolf. He was determined the creature should fall to his gun and was filled with a wild exultation at the thought. Obviously, the creature must be the leader of the pack.

The pack?

He halted.

What had come over him? It was madness for him to hunt for a wolf by night, madness to leave his children alone and unprotected.

Hastily he turned, and just as he started to retrace his steps, he heard a terrified cry.

"Help! Help! Oh, help me!"

"Who is it?" he shouted. "Where are you?"

"I am here. Close by. Oh, help me."

Holding up his lantern, he saw a fur-clad figure stumbling through the trees toward him.

"The wolves—the wolves have followed me all night and will not let me be. Oh, save me, forester, please save me, for I am all alone now and fear I can struggle no farther."

Startled, the forester looked down at the weeping woman and then stared around him, listening intently. Had he frightened away that white wolf and its pack?

"Come with me, lady," he said gruffly. "The sooner we are out of the forest the better." And, taking her arm, he hurried back following his own track, half dragging, half supporting her to where the firelight shone like a beacon through the kitchen window.

"Let me in, children," he called out as he approached the door. "I have a traveler with me who has just escaped from wolves."

He heard the heavy, wooden bars being drawn, and at last they were safe inside the warm kitchen.

With a sigh of exhaustion, the traveler sank in front of the fire, pulled off first her fur mittens and then her fur hat, and her hair fell to her waist in a cascade of palest gold.

As she shrugged herself free of her fur coat, the little boy, awakened by the arrival, sat up and stared at the woman in her richly embroidered dress, and reaching out a hand, touched the pale gold hair.

"Are you a princess?" he asked, and now he touched the velvet gown.

The lady smiled and held out her arms, and, as the boy hesitated, she leaned forward, lifted him onto her lap, and kissed him lightly on the brow.

"These are your children?" she asked, turning to the forester. "They are adorable." And she stretched out an arm to the daughter, but the little girl shrank away, busying herself with the fire, and pretending not to notice.

"Are you a princess?" the little boy repeated, and the lady shook her head and smiled sadly.

"There is a bed for you in the second room," the forester said. "I shall sleep here on the floor with the children. You will be safe with us."

"I am not tired yet," the lady said. "Let me stay here a while by the fire and watch the children sleep and do you keep me company."

The boy fell asleep at once but the girl was troubled and though she closed her eyes, sleep would not come. Soon she heard her father speak to the lady.

"Tomorrow, you must let me know what I can do to help you, for though you say you are not a princess, I know you must be a great lady, and I think you have never before been inside a cottage as humble as this."

"I am a lady and my father is rich, but in his castle I have never known such kindness as surrounds me here.

"My father wished me to marry a friend of his, an old man whom I feared and disliked. When he would not listen to my pleading, I offered my groom money and jewels if he would help me to escape and drive me to relations who are more understanding than my parents.

"He readily agreed. We set off last night, but in the snowstorm we lost our way. It was not long before a pack of wolves picked up our scent and began to follow us, knowing that soon the horses must tire. When one stumbled, my groom bade me jump and flee while he fought off the pack. Even as I protested, the leading horse fell and the sled with all my possessions and jewels overturned and I was thrown to one side. My head struck against a tree and I lost consciousness.

"When I recovered I was alone. Somehow the groom must have driven on, but far away I could hear the long drawn-out howling of the wolves and I knew . . . I knew . . ." She shivered. "To you I owe my life."

"Go to your bed now and sleep," the forester said. "There is nothing I or anyone can do tonight. But know that you can remain under my roof as long as you wish, and know that here you will always be safe."

That night, the little girl was awake long after everyone else was asleep, for she was filled with a fear she could not understand.

The next morning the forester set out for the place in the forest where he had encountered the lady, intent on tracing her sled and discovering the fate of her groom and horses. So heavily had the snow fallen, it had almost obliterated the tracks they had made the previous night but at last he reached a small clearing where the snow was churned and bore the deep prints of wolves and men: fresh snowflakes were settling on ugly brown stains which had recently been red.

"What the wolves did not devour, robbers have stolen," he said when he returned.

On hearing this, the lady wept bitterly.

"Alas! Now I have neither the means nor the money to continue my journey," she lamented. "What is to become of me?"

"Stay with us until summer comes, and then whatever you want to do, I shall help you," the forester said, whereupon the little boy hugged her, but the little girl turned away, wondering why the lady had no thought for the groom who had saved her life at the expense of his own.

During the day, the lady saw to the meals and the care of the cottage and played with the children, and the little boy loved her, but the little girl feared her and watched silently when her father came home and the lady waited on him and sat at his feet, and listened to him as he talked about his work and the people in the village in a way he had never talked to her or her brother.

With the coming of spring and the melting of the snow and ice, the lady wept again.

"I have been so happy here," she said, "and now I must leave you and I do not want to do that, for you three are dearer to me than my own relations."

"Then stay with us always," the forester begged. "Be my wife and the mother of my dear children." And the little girl saw that so infatuated was her father that in less than a year he had forgotten all about their real mother, and she feared the lady more than ever.

The next day, the forester and the lady went down into the village to visit the priest and to ask him to marry them, but there they found the old man had been taken ill very suddenly. However, another priest who happened to be passing, agreed to marry them there and then before continuing on his journey.

Delighted with his beautiful lady wife, the forester returned to his cottage, and though the little boy was nearly as happy as his father, the little girl was uneasy and afraid.

And with good reason. For now she was safely married, the lady sent the children to work in the fields all the time their father was away from home, and only when he returned did she make a pretence of speaking to them kindly.

"Let us tell our father how cruel she is to us," the boy whispered to his sister one day, for they had been sent out to work without anything to eat.

"Not yet. Have patience," his sister advised, and she gave him a stale crust that their stepmother had thrown out for the pig.

One night not long afterward, when the moon hung full in the sky, some sound awakened the girl, and she saw her stepmother, barefooted, and clothed only in a long, white nightgown, open the door, and then through the window, she watched her run from the cottage and down the silent village street.

Trembling, she lay down again and waited and just before daybreak, she saw her stepmother return, her hands and nightgown stained and red with what could only be blood. Horrified, she watched as the lady took off the nightgown, placed it on the fire, and watched it burn: after that she washed her hands, threw the water away, and then crept into the bed where her husband, the forester, slept so soundly.

A month later, when the moon was again full, the stepmother once more slipped out of the cottage, but this time

the girl followed her, for she remembered something she had heard in the village the previous day—how a young girl had unexpectedly died to the sorrow of her family, and she remembered, too, how four weeks before another young girl had died, the first such death for many months.

Keeping in the dark shadows, the girl hurried down the silent street; but just as the stepmother reached the churchyard, a cloud hid the moon and when the first beam shone down again, the lady had vanished and in her place stood a huge white wolf.

For a moment the creature stood motionless, sniffing the air, and then it bounded over the low wall and ran toward a recently filled grave, and began to dig with its forepaws.

Terrified, the girl turned and ran back home and lay shivering in bed. She was still awake, although she pretended to sleep when her stepmother returned just before daybreak, and again she watched as the lady burned her bloodstained nightgown and washed her hands.

When she told her brother what she had seen, he laughed. "That was a bad dream," he said, as they worked together in the fields. "How could our new mother have burned her nightgown when she has only one, and I can see it now hanging on the washing line?"

The girl stood up and looked across at the garment, and could not understand how this was so.

"Watch with me the next time after someone in the village has died and the moon is full," she begged.

"I will try to stay awake," he promised. "But I work so hard during the day that I fall asleep as soon as I crawl into bed. Waken me when the time comes."

Anxiously, the girl waited for news from the village and she sighed with relief when she knew that no one was ill and no one had died. This night I shall be able to sleep, she thought, taking a last look at the full moon, but soon a familiar sound wakened her, and she saw her stepmother slipping out of the door for the third time.

"Wake up! Wake up!" she urged, tugging at her brother's arm, but he slept on for all the world as though he were drugged.

And so she set off alone, keeping to the dark shadows of the silent street until she saw her stepmother stop outside the churchyard.

This time no cloud covered the moon.

This time she saw her stepmother tear off her nightgown and immediately change into a great white wolf, and she screamed out in fear and shrank back against the wall as the terrible creature leaped on her.

Awakened by that cry, the church verger flung open his window and leaned out.

"A wolf!" he shouted. "A great white wolf attacking a child!" And he discharged the gun he always kept ready to hand, whereupon the wolf dropped the girl, seized the nightgown between its teeth, and bounded away through the village.

"It is the forester's daughter and she must have been sleepwalking when the wolf attacked her," the verger's wife said. "How are we to tell her father?"

They carried the dead girl into their cottage, washed those savage bites, and dressed her in white, and they placed a single wild white flower in her clasped hands.

The following day, the girl was buried and the stepmother sobbed louder than anyone, louder even than the forester, but in the boy's eyes there was suspicion as well as grief.

Seven days later he went to the forge opposite the church, where the smith was busy as work.

"I have come to you for advice," he said, "for you are the wisest man in the village. All evil things fear you because of your power over cold and hot iron."

"What advice can I give you?" the smith asked.

"Two nights ago I had a dream," the boy said. "I dreamed that the moon was full and my sister went out and a big white werewolf attacked her and killed her. I woke and was afraid."

"Last night I dreamed again. Once more there was a full

moon and the white werewolf went hungry to the churchyard to dig up my sister and devour her."

"Have you told your father?" the smith asked.

"He would not believe me."

"Or the priest?"

"He is old and ill and would not understand."

"For a long time I have known there was evil in the village," the smith said slowly, "but until now I did not know how great that evil was. You did well to come to me for counsel."

"Return to your home and behave as though your grief was for a sister killed by accident. When next the moon is full, go to the forest where your father is working and ask him to come here with you as we are holding a solemn service in honor of his daughter. Do not let him return to his cottage."

"And you will protect my sister?"

"I give you my word that your sister, and indeed many others, will be protected."

From every man who stopped at the forge, the smith asked a silver coin, a silver button, or a piece of silver buckle or brooch, and everyone knew the reason and gave willingly: these tokens the smith melted down and made into a silver bullet.

The women, knowing what was afoot and aware of the peril in which they all stood, brought to the forge what bread and spirits they could spare.

On the night of the next full moon, all the men gathered in the forge and there the forester and his son joined them. Silently, they ate and drank. Silently, they waited.

It was nearly two hours later that they saw her running down the street, her pale, gold hair blowing in the wind, now covering and now revealing her lovely face, and so lightly did she move that her bare feet scarcely seemed to touch the ground.

The forester would have hurried out to her, but the others held him back.

"Wait," they murmured. "Wait and watch."

She had reached the churchyard now, and there she stopped, tore off her nightgown, and the next moment in her place stood a huge white wolf: lifting its head, it sniffed the air and then it bounded over the low wall, making for the place where the girl had been buried twenty-seven days previously.

"Now?" the men asked quietly.

"Now." the smith agreed, and lifting his gun to his shoulder, he took careful aim and fired, and the silver bullet penetrated the white fur and lodged in the creature's heart.

Lifting up its head for the last time, the werewolf gave one long, agonized howl and then collapsed. It was dead by the time the men reached it.

"I suspected nothing of this," the forester said. "I thought her beautiful and unfortunate. I took her into my home in her need, but she brought only evil and terror and death with her."

He helped the men bury the werewolf at a lonely place far from the village, and when they had set a huge stone over the grave, he took his son by the hand, and together they set off for a new life in some far-off village where no one would know of the cruel, white werewolf and the evil it had brought to innocent people.

# GETTING DEAD

*WILLIAM F. NOLAN*

H E'D BEEN TRYING to commit suicide for the past six thousand years. Off and on. No real pattern to it, just whenever he got really depressed about having to live forever, or when one of his straight friends died (for the most part, he found other vampires a gloomy lot and had always enjoyed outside, non-blood contacts.)

But suicide had never worked out for him. His will to survive, to live forever, was incredibly intense and fought against his sporadic attempts at self-extinction. He'd locked himself out of his castle several times and thrown away the key, figuring if he couldn't get inside to his casket before sunrise he'd be cooked to a fine, black ash. (He'd seen dozens of movies about vampires and always enjoyed it whenever the sun melted one of them.) Yet each time he locked himself he found a way to slip back into the damn castle . . . as a bat, or a wisp of smoke, or (twice) as a toad. His infernal shape-change ability invariably defeated these lock-out attempts.

Then, several times down the centuries, he devised ways to drive a stake through his heart . . . but never got it right. Helsinki: stake through his shoulder. London: stake through his upper thigh. Düsseldorf: stake through his left foot (he limped for six months), and so on. Never once in the heart. So he gave that up.

He tried boiled garlic in Yugoslavia. Prepared a tasty stew and had the garlic dumped in by a perverted dwarf pal of his. Devoured the entire bowl, belched, and sat back to die. But all he did was throw-up over the dwarf, who found the whole incident most disgusting.

In the Black Forest of Germany, he leaped from the roof of a village church onto a cross, ending up with some painful skin blisters where the cross had burned through his cape—but it didn't come *close* to killing him.

He drank a quart of holy water at Lourdes, resulting in a severe case of diarrhea.

And, naturally, he had talked several of his straight friends into attempting to kill him at various times, but either he killed them first, or they bungled the job.

So here he was, Count Arnold Whatever (he hadn't been able to remember his last name for the past seven hundred years), walking the night streets of Beverly Hills in the spring of 1991, determined to do away with himself but lacking a conclusive plan of action.

That was when he saw the ad.

It was block-painted on the wooden back of a bus-stop bench:

---

## ANYTHING, INC.

COME TO US IF ALL ELSE FAILS.
FOR THE PROPER FEE, WE'LL DO ANYTHING.
OPEN 24 HOURS!

WE'RE NEVER CLOSED TO *YOU*!

---

And the address was right there in Beverly Hills. On Rodeo Drive, near Wilshire.

Arnold was in a hurry, so he shape-changed and flapped over. He came through the office door as a bat (lots of screaming from the night secretary), and changed back into human form at the desk.

No appointment. He'd just flown in to demand service.

"Who the hell are you?" asked the tall man (he was flushed and balding) behind the desk of ANYTHING, INC.

"I am Count Arnold, and I am here to test the validity of your bus-stop advertisement—that, for the proper fee, you can do anything."

Mr. Anything (for that is how Arnold thought of him) settled back in his chair and lit a large, Cuban cigar. "I got two questions."

"So ask."

"What do you want done, and how much can you pay me to do it?"

"I want to stop being a vampire. And I will pay with these." Arnold produced a bag of emeralds and rubies, spilling the jewels across the desk.

Mr. Anything put a glass to his eye and examined each stone. That took ten full minutes. Then he looked up and smiled. "How old are you?"

"I am just a shade over ten thousand years old," said Arnold. "And for the first four thousand years I was content to be a vampire. Then I got bored. Then depressed. I have not been really happy for six thousand years."

Mr. Anything shifted his cigar. "I don't believe in vampires."

"I didn't either until I became one."

"Show me your teeth."

Arnold did. The two hollow, fangs, needle sharp, with which he sucked blood, were quite evident when he opened his mouth.

"You live off human blood?"

"That is correct."

"What's it taste like?"

"Depends. Most of the time it tastes fine. Then again,

I've had some that was downright bitter. But I never complain. I take it as it comes."

Mr. Anything got up from the desk, walked to the door, and closed it firmly. "*Prove* to me you're a vampire."

Arnold shrugged. "The only way to do that would be for me to suck all the blood from your body over a period of weeks—starting tonight."

"All right," said Mr. Anything with a note of sourness in his voice. "I'll take your word for it."

"I have tried literally everything to get rid of me," Arnold told him. "But I am very clever. I keep outsmarting myself, and just go on living. On and on and on. Living, living, living."

"I get your point," said the tall man.

"So . . . you have the jewels. They are worth a king's ransom. In fact, at one time in Bulgaria, they *were* a king's ransom, but that's neither here nor there. What I wish to know is," and Arnold leaned close to him, "how do you intend to dispose of me?"

Mr. Anything took a step back. "Your breath—"

"I know. It's fetid. There's just no way to keep it fresh." He frowned. "Well?"

"I could chain you to a post in full daylight and let the sun—"

"No, no, that's absolutely no good," said Arnold. "I'd just shape-change into a sewer rat and head for the nearest sewer. Sunlight's not the answer."

Mr. Anything paced the room, puffing out cannon bursts of cigar smoke. "I'm sure that a stake through the heart would—"

Arnold shook his head. "I've tried the stake thing over and over and I'm telling you it's a waste of time."

"C'mon, you gotta be kidding. You mean, even with you all snug in the coffin and me leaning over you with a big mallet to pound it into your chest while you sleep?"

"Won't work. Vampires are light sleepers. When we feel the point of a sharpened stake tickle our skin we jump." Arnold sighed. "I'd just reach up from the coffin and tear your throat out."

Mr. Anything thought that over. "Yeah . . . well, that would not be so good."

He kept pacing. Then he stopped, turned to Arnold, and clapped him on the shoulder. "I got it." He grinned. "Your troubles are over."

"Really?" Arnold looked skeptical.

"Believe me, you're as good as dead. I mean *dead* dead. My word on it."

And they shook hands.

A week later, on a clouded night, Arnold woke up. Mr. Anything had obviously used some kind of drug on him. So he couldn't shape-change.

His neck was sore.

He reached up to touch it. Something had bitten him. The wound was newly infected; there was blood on his fingertips.

This was stupid. You don't kill a vampire by having another vampire bite him (or her). That's how it all starts in the first place.

He felt the wound again. Multiple teeth bites—not just the usual twin fang marks.

Something else had bitten him . . . *changed* him.

The clouds parted and the moon was full.

Hair was sprouting out of skin in rough, brown clumps. And he felt his jaw lengthen.

Arnold howled.

And he happened to be knowledgable enough about the real world of Night Creatures to know that a silver bullet was totally ineffectual.

Damn!

# THE ADVENTURE OF THE
# SUSSEX VAMPIRE

*ARTHUR CONAN DOYLE*

HOLMES HAD READ CAREFULLY a note which the last post had brought him. Then, with the dry chuckle which was his nearest approach to a laugh, he tossed it over to me.

"For a mixture of the modern and the medieval, of the practical and of the wildly fanciful, I think this is surely the limit," said he. "What do you make of it, Watson?"

I read as follows:

46 OLD JEWRY,
Nov. 19th

*Re:* Vampires

SIR,
Our client, Mr. Robert Ferguson, of Ferguson and Muirhead, tea brokers of Mincing Lane, has made some inquiry from us in a communication of even date concerning vampires. As our firm specializes entirely

upon the assessment of machinery, the matter hardly comes without our purview, and we have therefore recommended Mr. Ferguson to call upon you and lay the matter before you. We have not forgotten your successful action in the case of Matilda Briggs.

We are, Sir,

Faithfully yours,

MORRISON, MORRISON, AND DODD
per E.J.C.

"Matilda Briggs was not the name of a young woman, Watson," said Holmes in a reminiscent voice. "It was a ship which is associated with the giant rat of Sumatra, a story for which the world is not yet prepared. But what do we know about vampires? Does it come within our purview either? Anything is better than stagnation, but really we seem to have been switched on to a Grimm's fairy tale. Make a long arm, Watson, and see what 'V' has to say."

I leaned back and took down the great index volume to which he referred. Holmes balanced it on his knee, and his eyes moved slowly and lovingly over the record of old cases, mixed with the accumulated information of a lifetime.

"Voyage of the *Gloria Scott*," he read. "That was a bad business. I have some recollection that you made a record of it, Watson, though I was unable to congratulate you upon the result. Victor Lunch, the forger. Venomous lizard or gila. Remarkable case, that! Vittoria, the circus belle. Vanderbilt and the Yeggman. Vipers, Vogir, the Hammersmith wonder. Hello! Hello! Good old index. You can't beat it. Listen to this, Watson. Vampirism in Hungary. And again, Vampires in Transylvania." He turned over the pages with eagerness, but after a short intent perusal he threw down the great book with a snarl of disappointment.

"Rubbish, Watson, rubbish! What have we to do with

walking corpses who can only be held in their grave by stakes driven through their hearts? It's pure lunacy."

"But surely," said I, "the vampire was not necessarily a dead man? A living person might have the habit. I have read, for example, of the old sucking the blood of the young in order to retain their youth."

"You are right, Watson. It mentions the legend in one of these references. But are we to give serious attention to such things? This Agency stands flat-footed upon the ground, and there it must remain. The world is big enough for us. No ghosts need apply. I fear that we cannot take Mr. Robert Ferguson very seriously. Possibly this note may be from him, and may throw some light upon what is worrying him."

He took up a second letter which had lain unnoticed upon the table while he had been absorbed with the first. This he began to read with a smile of amusement upon his face which gradually faded away into an expression of intense interest and concentration. When he had finished he sat for some little time lost in thought with the letter dangling from his fingers. Finally, with a start, he aroused himself from his reverie.

"Cheeseman's, Lamberley. Where is Lamberley, Watson?"

"It is in Sussex, south of Horsham."

"Not very far, eh? And Cheeseman's?"

"I know that country, Holmes. It is full of old houses which are named after the men who built them centuries ago. You get Odley's and Harvey's and Carriton's—the folk are forgotten, but their names live in their houses."

"Precisely," said Holmes coldly. It was one of the peculiarities of his proud, self-contained nature that, though he docketed any fresh information very quietly and accurately in his brain, he seldom made any acknowledgment to the giver. "I rather fancy we shall know a good deal more about Cheeseman's, Lamberley, before we are through. The letter is, as I had hoped, from Robert Ferguson. By the way, he claims acquaintance with you."

"With me!"

"You had better read it."

He handed the letter across. It was headed with the address quoted.

DEAR MR. HOLMES, [it said]

I have been recommended to you by my lawyers, but indeed the matter is so extraordinarily delicate that it is most difficult to discuss. It concerns a friend for whom I am acting. This gentleman married some five years ago a Peruvian lady, the daughter of a Peruvian merchant, whom he had met in connection with the importation of nitrates. The lady was very beautiful, but the fact of her foreign birth and of her alien religion always caused a separation of interests and of feelings between husband and wife, so that after a time his love may have cooled toward her, and he may have come to regard their union as a mistake. He felt there were sides of her character which he could never explore or understand. This was the more painful as she was as loving a wife as a man could have—to all appearance, absolutely devoted.

Now for the point which I will make more plain when we meet. Indeed, this note is merely to give you a general idea of the situation and to ascertain whether you would care to interest yourself in the matter. The lady began to show some curious traits quite alien to her ordinarily sweet and gentle disposition. The gentleman had been married twice and he had one son by the first wife. This boy was now fifteen, a very charming and affectionate youth, though unhappily injured through an accident in childhood. Twice the wife was caught in the act of assaulting this poor lad in the most unprovoked way. Once she struck him with a stick and left a great weal on his arm.

This was a small matter, however, compared with the conduct to her own child, a dear boy just under one year of age. On one occasion about a month ago, this child had been left by its nurse for a few minutes.

A loud cry from the baby, as of pain, called the nurse back. As she ran into the room she saw her employer, the lady, leaning over the baby and apparently biting his neck. There was a small wound in the neck, from which a stream of blood had escaped. The nurse was so horrified that she wished to call the husband, but the lady implored her not to do so, and actually gave her five pounds as a price for her silence. No explanation was ever given, and, for the moment, the matter was passed over.

It left, however, a terrible impression upon the nurse's mind, and from that time she began to watch her mistress closely, and to keep a closer guard upon the baby, whom she tenderly loved. It seemed to her that even as she watched the mother, so the mother watched her, and that every time she was compelled to leave the baby alone the mother was waiting to get at it. Day and night the nurse covered the child, and day and night the silent, watchful mother seemed to be lying in wait as a wolf waits for a lamb. It must read most incredible to you, and yet I beg you to take it seriously, for a child's life and a man's sanity may depend upon it.

At last there came one dreadful day when the facts could no longer be concealed from the husband. The nurse's nerve had given way; she could stand the strain no longer, and she made a clean breast of it all to the man. To him it seemed as wild a tale as it may now seem to you. He knew his wife to be a loving wife, and, save for the assaults upon her stepson, a loving mother. Why, then, should she wound her own dear little baby? He told the nurse that she was dreaming, that her suspicions were those of a lunatic, and that such libels upon her mistress were not to be tolerated. While they were talking, a sudden cry of pain was heard. Nurse and master rushed together to the nursery. Imagine his feelings, Mr. Holmes, as he saw

his wife rise from a kneeling position beside the cot, and saw blood upon the child's exposed neck and upon the sheet. With a cry of horror, he turned his wife's face to the light and saw blood all around her lips. It was she—she beyond all question—who had drunk the poor baby's blood.

So the matter stands. She is now confined to her room. There has been no explanation. The husband is half demented. He knows, and I know, little of vampirism beyond the name. We had thought it was some wild tale of foreign parts. And yet here in the very heart of English Sussex—well, all this can be discussed with you in the morning. Will you see me? Will you use your great powers in aiding a distracted man? If so, kindly wire to Ferguson, Cheeseman's, Lamberley, and I will be at your rooms by ten o'clock.

Yours faithfully,

ROBERT FERGUSON

P.S. I believe your friend Watson played Rugby for Blackheath when I was three-quarter for Richmond. It is the only personal introduction which I can give.

"Of course I remember him," said I, as I laid down the letter. "Big Bob Ferguson, the finest three-quarter Richmond ever had. He was always a good-natured chap. It's like him to be so concerned over a friend's case."

Holmes looked at me thoughtfully and shook his head.

"I never get your limits, Watson," said he. "There are unexplored possibilities about you. Take a wire down, like a good fellow. 'Will examine your case with pleasure.'"

"*Your* case!"

"We must not let him think that this Agency is a home for the weak-minded. Of course it is his case. Send him that wire and let the matter rest till morning."

*

Promptly at ten o'clock next morning, Ferguson strode into our room. I had remembered him as a long, slab-sided man with loose limbs and a fine turn of speed, which had carried him around many an opposing back. There is surely nothing in life more painful than to meet the wreck of a fine athlete whom one has known in his prime. His great frame had fallen in, his flaxen hair was scanty, and his shoulders were bowed. I fear that I roused corresponding emotions in him.

"Hello, Watson," said he, and his voice was still deep and hearty. "You don't look quite the man you did when I threw you over the ropes into the crowd at the Old Deer Park. I expect I have changed a bit also. But it's this last day or two that has aged me. I see by your telegram, Mr. Holmes, that it is no use my pretending to be anyone's deputy."

"It is simpler to deal direct," said Holmes.

"Of course it is. But you can imagine how difficult it is when you are speaking of the one woman you are bound to protect and help. What can I do? How am I to go to the police with such a story? And yet the kiddies have got to be protected. Is it madness, Mr. Holmes? Is it something in the blood? Have you any similar case in your experience? For God's sake, give me some advice, for I am at my wit's end."

"Very naturally, Mr. Ferguson. Now sit here and pull yourself together and give me a few clear answers. I can assure you that I am far from being at my wit's end, and that I am confident we shall find some solution. First of all, tell me what steps you have taken. Is your wife still near the children?"

"We had a dreadful scene. She is a most loving woman, Mr. Holmes. If ever a woman loved a man with all her heart and soul, she loves me. She was cut to the heart that I should have discovered this horrible, this incredible, secret. She would not even speak. She gave no answer to my reproaches, save to gaze at me with a wild, despairing look in her eyes. Then she rushed to her room and locked herself in. Since then she has refused to see me. She has a maid who was with her before her marriage, Dolores by name—a friend rather than a servant. She takes her food to her."

"Then the child is in no immediate danger?"

"Mrs. Mason, the nurse, has sworn that she will not leave it night or day. I can absolutely trust her. I am more uneasy about poor little Jack, for, as I told you in my note, he has twice been assaulted by her."

"But never wounded?"

"No, she struck him savagely. It is the more terrible as he is a poor little inoffensive cripple." Ferguson's gaunt features softened as he spoke of his boy. "You would think that the dear lad's condition would soften anyone's heart. A fall in childhood and a twisted spine, Mr. Holmes. But the dearest, most loving heart within."

Holmes had picked up the letter of yesterday and was reading it over. "What other inmates are there in your house, Mr. Ferguson?"

"Two servants who have not been long with us. One stablehand, Michael, who sleeps in the house. My wife, myself, my boy Jack, baby, Dolores, and Mrs. Mason. That is all."

"I gather that you did not know your wife well at the time of your marriage?"

"I had only known her a few weeks."

"How long had this maid Dolores been with her?"

"Some years."

"Then your wife's character would really be better known by Dolores than by you?"

"Yes, you may say so."

Holmes made a note.

"I fancy," said he, "that I may be of more use at Lamberley than here. It is eminently a case for personal investigation. If the lady remains in her room, our presence could not annoy or inconvenience her. Of course, we would stay at the inn."

Ferguson gave a gesture of relief.

"It is what I hoped, Mr. Holmes. There is an excellent train at two from Victoria, if you could come."

"Of course we could come. There is a lull at present. I can give you my undivided energies. Watson, of course, comes with us. But there are one or two points upon which I wish to be very sure before I start. This unhappy lady, as I understand it, has appeared to assault both the children, her own baby, and your little son."

"That is so."

"But the results take different forms, do they not? She has beaten your son."

"Once with a stick and once very savagely with her hands."

"Did she give no explanation why she struck him?"

"None, save that she hated him. Again and again she said so."

"Well, that is not unknown among stepmothers. A posthumous jealousy, we will say. Is the lady jealous by nature?"

"Yes, she is very jealous—jealous with all the strength of her fiery, tropical love."

"But the boy—he is fifteen, I understand, and probably very developed in mind, since his body has been circumscribed in action. Did he give you no explanation of these assaults?"

"No; he declared there was no reason."

"Were they good friends at other times?"

"No; there was never any love between them."

"Yet you say he is affectionate?"

"Never in the world could there be so devoted a son. My life is his life. He is absorbed in what I say or do."

Once again Holmes made a note. For some time he sat lost in thought.

"No doubt you and the boy were great comrades before this second marriage. You were thrown very close together, were you not?"

"Very much so."

"And the boy, having so affectionate a nature, was devoted, no doubt, to the memory of his mother?"

"Most devoted."

"He would certainly seem to be a most interesting lad.

There is one other point about these assaults. Were the strange attacks upon the baby and the assaults upon your son at the same period?"

"In her first case it was so. It was as if some frenzy had seized her, and she had vented her rage upon both. In the second case it was only Jack who suffered. Mrs. Mason had no complaint to make about the baby."

"That certainly complicates matters."

"I don't quite follow you, Mr. Holmes."

"Possibly not. One forms provisional theories and waits for time or fuller knowledge to explode them. A bad habit, Mr. Ferguson; but human nature is weak. I fear that your old friend here has given an exaggerated view of my scientific methods. However, I will only say at the present stage that your problem does not appear to me to be insoluble, and that you may expect to find us at Victoria at two o'clock."

It was evening of a dull, foggy, November day when, having left our bags at the Chequers, Lamberley, we drove through the Sussex clay of a long, winding lane and finally reached the isolated and ancient farmhouse in which Ferguson dwelled. It was a large, straggling building, very old in the center, very new at the wings, with towering Tudor chimneys and a lichen-spotted, high-pitched roof of Horsham slabs. The doorsteps were worn into curves, and the ancient tiles which lined the porch were marked with the rebus of a cheese and a man, after the original builder. Within, the ceilings were corrugated with heavy oaken beams, and the uneven floors sagged into sharp curves. An odor of age and decay pervaded the whole crumbling building.

There was one very large, central room into which Ferguson led us. Here, in a huge, old-fashioned fireplace with an iron screen behind it dated 1670, there blazed and spluttered a splendid log fire.

The room, as I gazed around, was a most singular mixture of dates and of places. The half-paneled walls may well have belonged to the original yeoman farmer of the seventeenth century. They were ornamented, however, on the lower part by a line of well-chosen modern water-colors; while above, where yellow plaster took the place of oak, there was hung a fine collection of South American utensils and weapons, which had been brought, no doubt, by the Peruvian lady upstairs. Holmes rose, with that quick curiosity which sprang from his eager mind, and examined them with some care. He returned with his eyes full of thought.

"Hello!" he cried. "Hello!"

A spaniel had lain in a basket in the corner. It came slowly forward toward its master, walking with difficulty. Its hind legs moved irregularly and its tail was on the ground. It licked Ferguson's hand.

"What is it, Mr. Holmes?"

"The dog. What's the matter with it?"

"That's what puzzled the vet. A sort of paralysis. Spinal meningitis, he thought. But it is passing. He'll be all right soon —won't you, Carlo?"

A shiver of assent passed through the drooping tail. The dog's mournful eyes passed from one of us to the other. He knew that we were discussing his case.

"Did it come on suddenly?"

"In a single night."

"How long ago?"

"It may have been four months ago."

"Very remarkable. Very suggestive."

"What do you see in it, Mr. Holmes?"

"A confirmation of what I had already thought."

"For God's sake, what *do* you think, Mr. Holmes? It may be a mere intellectual puzzle to you, but it is life and death to me! My wife a would-be murderer—my child in constant danger! Don't play with me, Mr. Holmes. It is too terribly serious."

The big rugby three-quarter was trembling all over. Holmes put his hand soothingly upon his arm.

"I fear that there is pain for you, Mr. Ferguson, whatever the solution may be," said he. "I would spare you all I can. I cannot say more for the instant, but before I leave this house

I hope I may have something definite."

"Please God you may! If you will excuse me, gentlemen, I will go up to my wife's room and see if there has been any change."

He was away some minutes; during which Holmes resumed his examination of the curiosities upon the wall. When our host returned it was clear from his downcast face that he had made no progress. He brought with him a tall, slim girl.

"The tea is ready, Dolores," said Ferguson. "See that your mistress has everything she can wish."

"She verra ill," cried the girl, looking with indignant eyes at her master. "She no ask for food. She verra ill. She need doctor. I frightened stay alone with her without doctor."

Ferguson looked at me with a question in his eyes.

"I should be so glad if I could be of use."

"Would your mistress see Dr. Watson?"

"I take him. I no ask leave. She needs doctor."

"Then I'll come with you at once."

I followed the girl, who was quivering with strong emotion, up the staircase and down an ancient corridor. At the end was an iron-clamped and massive door. It struck me as I looked at it that if Ferguson tried to force his way to his wife, he would find it no easy matter. The girl drew a key from her pocket, and the heavy oaken planks creaked upon their old hinges. I passed in and she swiftly followed, fastening the door behind her.

On the bed, a woman was lying who was clearly in a high fever. She was only half conscious, but as I entered she raised a pair of frightened but beautiful eyes and glared at me in apprehension. Seeing a stranger, she appeared to be relieved, and sank back with a sigh upon the pillow. I stepped up to her with a few reassuring words, and she lay still while I took her pulse and temperature. Both were high, and yet my impression was the condition was rather that of mental and nervous excitement than of any actual seizure.

"She lie like that one day, two day. I 'fraid she die," said the girl.

The woman turned her flushed and handsome face toward me.

"Where is my husband?"

"He is below, and would wish to see you."

"I will not see him. I will not see him." Then she seemed to wander off into delirium. "A fiend! A fiend! Oh, what shall I do with this devil?"

"Can I help you in any way?"

"No. No one can help. It is finished. All is destroyed. Do what I will, all is destroyed."

The woman must have some strange delusion. I could not see honest Bob Ferguson in the character of fiend or devil.

"Madame," I said, "your husband loves you dearly. He is deeply grieved at this happening."

Again she turned on me those glorious eyes.

"He loves me. Yes. But do I not love him? Do I not love him even to sacrifice myself rather than break his dear heart? That is how I love him. And yet he could think of me—he could speak to me so."

"He is full of grief, but he cannot understand."

"No, he cannot understand. But he should trust."

"Will you not see him?" I suggested.

"No, no. I cannot forget those terrible words nor the look upon his face. I will not see him. Go now. You can do nothing for me. Tell him only one thing. I want my child. I have a right to my child. That is the only message I can send him." She turned her face to the wall and would say no more.

I returned to the room downstairs, where Ferguson and Holmes still sat by the fire. Ferguson listened moodily to my account of the interview.

"How can I send her the child?" he said. "How do I know what strange impulse might come upon her? How can I ever forget how she rose from beside it with its blood on her lips?" He shuddered at the recollection. "The child is safe with Mrs. Mason, and there he must remain."

A smart maid, the only modern thing which we had seen in the house, had brought in some tea. As she was serving it, the door opened and a youth entered the room. He was a remarkable lad, pale-faced and fair-haired, with excitable light-blue eyes which blazed into a sudden flame of emotion and joy as they rested upon his father. He rushed forward and threw his arms around his neck with the abandon of a loving girl.

"Oh, Daddy," he cried. "I did not know that you were due yet. I should have been here to meet you. Oh, I am so glad to see you!"

Ferguson gently disengaged himself from the embrace with some little show of embarrassment.

"Dear old chap," said he, patting the flaxen head with a very tender hand. "I come early because my friends, Mr. Holmes and Dr. Watson, have been persuaded to come down and spend an evening with us."

"Is that Mr. Holmes, the detective?"

"Yes."

The youth looked at us with a very penetrating and, as it seemed to me, unfriendly gaze.

"What about your other child, Mr. Ferguson?" asked Holmes. "Might we make the acquaintance of the baby?"

"Ask Mrs. Mason to bring baby down," said Ferguson. The boy went off with a curious, shambling gait which told my surgical eyes that he was suffering from a weak spine. Presently he returned, and behind him came a tall, gaunt woman bearing in her arms a very beautiful child, dark-eyed, golden-haired, a wonderful mixture of the Saxon and the Latin. Ferguson was evidently devoted to it, for he took it into his arms and fondled it most tenderly.

"Fancy anyone having the heart to hurt him," he muttered, as he glanced down at the small, angry red pucker upon the cherub throat.

It was at this moment that I chanced to glance at Holmes, and saw a most singular intentness in his expression. His face was as set as if it had been carved out of old ivory, and his eyes, which had glanced for a moment at father and child, were now fixed with eager curiosity upon something at the

110

other side of the room. Following his gaze, I could only guess that he was looking out through the window at the melancholy, dripping garden. It is true that a shutter had half closed outside and obstructed the view, but nonetheless it was certainly at the window that Holmes was fixing his concentrated attention. Then he smiled, and his eyes came back to the baby. On its chubby neck there was this small puckered mark. Without speaking, Holmes examined it with care. Finally, he shook one of the dimpled fists which waved in front of him.

"Goodbye, little man. You have made a strange start in life. Nurse, I should wish to have a word with you in private."

He took her aside and spoke earnestly for a few minutes. I only heard the last words, which were: "Your anxiety will soon, I hope, be set at rest." The woman, who seemed to be a sour, silent kind of creature, withdrew with the child.

"What is Mrs. Mason like?" asked Holmes.

"Not very prepossessing externally, as you can see, but a heart of gold, and devoted to the child."

"Do you like her, Jack?" Holmes turned suddenly upon the boy. His expressive mobile face shadowed over, and he shook his head.

"Jacky has very strong likes and dislikes," said Ferguson, putting his arm around the boy. "Luckily I am one of his likes."

The boy cooed and nestled his head upon his father's breast. Ferguson gently disengaged him.

"Run away, little Jacky," said he, and he watched his son with loving eyes until he disappeared. "Now, Mr. Holmes," he continued, when the boy was gone. "I really feel that I have brought you on a fool's errand, for what can you possibly do, save give your sympathy? It must be an exceedingly delicate and complex affair from your point of view."

"It is certainly delicate," said my friend with an amused smile, "but I have not been struck up to now with its complexity. It has been a case for intellectual deduction, but when this original intellectual deduction is confirmed point by point by quite a number of independent incidents, then the subjective becomes objective and we can say confidently that we have reached our goal. I had, in fact, reached it before we left Baker Street, and the rest has merely been observation and confirmation."

Ferguson put his big hand to his furrowed forehead.

"For Heaven's sake, Holmes," he said hoarsely, "if you can see the truth in this matter, do not keep me in suspense. How do I stand? What shall I do? I care nothing as to how you have found your facts so long as you have really got them."

"Certainly, I owe you an explanation, and you shall have it. But you will permit me to handle the matter in my own way? Is the lady capable of seeing us, Watson?"

"She is ill, but she is quite rational."

"Very good. It is only in her presence that we can clear the matter up. Let us go up to her."

"She will not see me," cried Ferguson.

"Oh, yes, she will," said Holmes. He scribbled a few lines upon a sheet of paper. "You at least have the entrée, Watson. Will you have the goodness to give the lady this note?"

I ascended again and handed the note to Dolores, who cautiously opened the door. A minute later I heard a cry from within, a cry in which joy and surprise seemed to be blended. Dolores looked out.

"She will see them. She will leesten," said she.

At my summons, Ferguson and Holmes came up. As we entered the room Ferguson took a step or two toward his wife, who had raised herself in the bed, but she held out her hand to repulse him. He sank into an armchair, while Holmes seated himself beside him, after bowing to the lady, who looked at him with wide-eyed amazement.

"I think we can dispense with Dolores," said Holmes. "Oh, very well, madame, if you would rather she stayed I can see no objection. Now, Mr. Ferguson, I am a busy man with many calls, and my methods have to be short and direct. The swiftest surgery is the least painful. Let me first say what will ease your mind. Your wife is a very good, a very loving, and a very ill-used woman."

Ferguson sat up with a cry of joy.

"Prove that, Mr. Holmes, and I am your debtor forever."

"I will do so, but in doing so I must wound you deeply in another direction."

"I care nothing so long as you clear my wife. Everything on earth is insignificant compared to that."

"Let me tell you, then, the train of reasoning which passed through my mind in Baker Street. The idea of a vampire was to me absurd. Such things do not happen in criminal practice in England. And yet your observation was precise. You had seen the lady rise from beside the child's cot with the blood upon her lips."

"I did."

"Did it not occur to you that a bleeding wound may be sucked for some other purpose than to draw the blood from it? Was there not a queen in English history who sucked such a wound to draw poison from it?"

"Poison!"

"A South American household. My instinct felt the presence of those weapons upon the wall before my eyes ever saw them. It might have been other poison, but that was what occurred to me. When I saw that little empty quiver beside the small bird-bow, it was just what I expected to see. If the child were pricked with one of those arrows dipped in curare or some other devilish drug, it would mean death if the venom were not sucked out.

"And the dog! If one were to use such a poison, would one not try it first in order to see that it had not lost its power? I did not foresee the dog, but at least I understand him and he fitted into my reconstruction.

"Now do you understand? Your wife feared such an attack. She saw it made and saved the child's life, and yet she shrank from telling you all the truth, for she knew how you loved the boy and feared lest it break your heart."

"Jacky!"

"I watched him as you fondled the child just now. His face was clearly reflected in the glass of the window where the shutter formed a background. I saw such jealousy, such cruel hatred, as I have seldom seen in a human face."

"My Jacky!"

"You have to face it, Mr. Ferguson. It is the more painful because it is a distorted love, a maniacal exaggerated love for you, and possibly for his dead mother, which has prompted his action. His very soul is consumed with hatred for this splendid child, whose health and beauty are a contrast to his own weakness."

"Good God! It is incredible!"

"Have I spoken the truth, madame?"

The lady was sobbing, with her face buried in the pillows. Now she turned to her husband.

"How could I tell you, Bob? I felt the blow it would be to you. It was better that I should wait and that it should come from some other lips than mine. When this gentleman, who seems to have powers of magic, wrote that he knew all, I was glad."

"I think a year at sea would be my prescription for Master Jacky," said Holmes, rising from his chair. "Only one thing is still clouded, madame. We can quite understand your attacks upon Master Jacky. There is a limit to a mother's patience. But how did you dare to leave the child these last two days?"

"I had told Mrs. Mason. She knew."

"Exactly. So I imagined."

Ferguson was standing by the bed, choking, his hands outstretched and quivering.

"This, I fancy, is the time for our exit, Watson," said Holmes in a whisper. "If you will take one elbow of the too faithful Dolores, I will take the other. There, now," he added, as he closed the door behind him, "I think we may leave them to settle the rest among themselves."

I have only one further note in this case. It is the letter which Holmes wrote in final answer to that with which the narrative begins. It ran thus:

BAKER STREET,

Nov. 21st

*Re:* Vampires

SIR,

Referring to your letter of the 19th, I beg to state that I have looked into the inquiry of your client, Mr. Robert Ferguson, of Ferguson and Muirhead, tea brokers of Mincing Lane, and that the matter has been brought to a satisfactory conclusion. With thanks for your recommendation, I am, Sir,

Faithfully yours,

SHERLOCK HOLMES

# THE WEREWOLF

*CLEMENCE HOUSMAN*

*Clemence Housman was the sister of the famous poet A. E. Housman.
"The Werewolf" may be the only thing of note that she wrote, but
it's as thrilling a tale as any you're ever likely to read. It's the story
of devoted brothers Sweyn and Christian, who become bitterly
divided over the mysterious White Fell. Sweyn is bewitched by her
beauty, but Christian sees her at once for what she really is: a
predatory werewolf looking for victims. But how can he make his
brother see the truth? Eventually he decides he must pursue White
Fell and confront her when she turns from woman to beast,
whatever the danger to himself . . .*

:

SHE CAME WITH A SMOOTH, gliding, noiseless speed, that
was neither walking nor running; her arms were folded
in her furs that were drawn tight around her body: the
white lappets from her head were wrapped and knotted
closely beneath her face; her eyes were set on a far distance. So
she went till the even sway of her going was startled to a
pause by Christian.

"Fell!"

She drew a quick, sharp breath at the sound of her name
thus mutilated, and faced Sweyn's brother. Her eyes glittered;

her upper lip was lifted, and showed the teeth. The half of her name, impressed with an ominous sense as uttered by him, warned her of the aspect of a deadly foe. Yet she cast loose her robes till they trailed ample, and spoke as a mild woman.

"What would you?"

Then Christian answered with his solemn, dreadful accusation:

"You kissed Rol—and Rol is dead! You kissed Trella: she is dead! You have kissed Sweyn, my brother; but he shall not die!"

He added: "You may live till midnight."

The edge of the teeth and the glitter of the eyes stayed a moment, and her right hand also slid down to the ax handle. Then, without a word, she swerved from him, and sprang out and away swiftly over the snow.

And Christian sprang out and away, and followed her swiftly over the snow, keeping behind, but half-a-stride's length from her side.

So they went running together, silent, toward the vast wastes of snow, where no living thing but they two moved under the stars of night.

Never before had Christian so rejoiced in his powers. The gift of speed, and the training of use and endurance, were priceless to him now. Though midnight was hours away, he was confident that, go where that Fell Thing would, hasten as she would, she could not outstrip him nor escape from him. Then, when came the time for transformation, when the woman's form made no longer a shield against a man's hand, he could slay or be slain to save Sweyn. He had struck his dear brother in dire extremity, but he could not, though reason urged, strike a woman.

For one mile, for two miles they ran: White Fell ever foremost, Christian ever at equal distance from her side, so near that, now and again, her out-flying furs touched him. She spoke no word; nor he. She never turned her head to look at him, nor swerved to evade him; but, with set face looking forward, sped straight on, over rough, over smooth, aware of his nearness by the regular beat of his feet, and the sound of his breath behind.

In a while, she quickened her pace. From the first, Christian had judged of her speed as admirable, yet with exulting security in his own excelling and enduring, whatever her efforts. But, when the pace increased, he found himself put to the test as never had he been before in any race. Her feet, indeed, flew faster than his; it was only by his length of stride that he kept his place at her side. But his heart was high and resolute, and he did not fear failure yet.

So the desperate race flew on. Their feet struck up the powdery snow, their breath smoked into the sharp clear air, and they were gone before the air was cleared of snow and vapor. Now and then Christian glanced up to judge, by the rising of the stars, of the coming of midnight. So long—so long!

While Fell held on without slack. She, it was evident, with confidence in her speed proving matchless, as resolute to outrun her pursuer as he to endure till midnight and fulfil his purpose. And Christian held on, still self-assured. He could not fail; he would not fail. To avenge Rol and Trella was motive enough for him to do what man could do; but for Sweyn more. She had kissed Sweyn, but he should not die too: with Sweyn to save he could not fail.

Never before was such a race as this; no, not when in old Greece man and maid raced together with two fates at stake; for the hard running was sustained unabated, while star after star rose and went wheeling up toward midnight, for one hour, for two hours.

Then Christian saw and heard what shot him through with fear. Where a fringe of trees hung around a slope, he saw something dark moving, and heard a yelp, followed by a full horrid cry, and the dark spread out upon the snow, a pack of wolves in pursuit.

Of the beasts alone he had little cause for fear; at the pace he held he could distance them, four-footed though they were. But of White Fell's wiles he had infinite apprehension, for

how might she not avail herself of the savage jaws of these wolves, akin as they were to half her nature. She vouchsafed to them nor look nor sign; but Christian, on an impulse to assure himself that she should not escape him, caught and held the back-flung edge of her furs, running still.

She turned like a flash with a beastly snarl, teeth and eyes gleaming again. Her ax shone, on the upstroke, on the downstroke, as she hacked at his hand. She had lopped it off at the wrist, but that he parried with the bear spear. Even then, she shore through the shaft and shattered the bones of the hand at the same blow, so that he loosed perforce.

Then again they raced on as before, Christian not losing a pace, though his left hand swung useless, bleeding and broken.

The snarl, indubitable, though modified from a woman's organs, the vicious fury revealed in teeth and eyes, the sharp arrogant pain of her maiming blow, caught away Christian's heed of the beasts behind, by striking into him close vivid realization of the infinitely greater danger that ran before him in that deadly Thing.

When he bethought him to look behind, lo! the pack had but reached their tracks, and instantly slunk aside, cowed; the yell of pursuit changing to yelps and whines. So abhorrent was that fell creature to beast as to man.

She had drawn her furs more closely to her, disposing them so that, instead of flying loose to her heels, no drapery hung lower than her knees, and this without a check to her wonderful speed, nor embarrassment by the cumbering of the folds. She held her head as before; her lips were firmly set, only the tense nostrils gave her breath; not a sign of distress witnessed to the long sustaining of that terrible speed.

But on Christian by now the strain was telling palpably. His head weighed heavy, and his breath came laboring in great sobs; the bear spear would have been a burden now. His heart was beating like a hammer, but such a dullness oppressed his brain, that it was only by degrees he could realize his helpless state; wounded and weaponless, chasing that terrible Thing, that was a fierce, desperate, ax-armed woman, except she should assume the beast with fangs yet more formidable.

And still the far, slow stars went lingering nearly an hour from midnight.

So far was his brain astray that an impression took him that she was fleeing from the midnight stars, whose gain was by such slow degrees that a time equaling days and days had gone in the race around the northern circle of the world, and days and days as long might last before the end—except she slackened, or except he failed.

But he would not fail yet.

How long had he been praying so? He had started with a self-confidence and reliance that had felt no need for that aid; and now it seemed the only means by which to restrain his heart from swelling beyond the compass of his body, by which to cherish his brain from dwindling and shriveling quite away. Some sharp-toothed creature kept tearing and dragging on his maimed left hand; he never could see it, he could not shake it off, but he prayed it off at times.

The clear stars before him took to shuddering, and he knew why; they shuddered at sight of what was behind him. He had never divined before that strange things hid themselves from men under pretense of being snow-clad mounds or swaying trees; but now they came slipping out from their harmless covers to follow him, and mock at his impotence to make a kindred Thing resolve to truer form. He knew the air behind him was thronged; he heard the hum of innumerable murmurings together; but his eyes could never catch them, they were too swift and nimble. Yet he knew they were there, because, on a backward glance, he saw the snow mounds surge as they groveled flatlings out of sight; he saw the trees reel as they screwed themselves rigid past recognition among the boughs.

And after such glance, the stars for awhile returned to steadfastness, and an infinite stretch of silence froze upon the chill gray world, only deranged by the swift even beat of the flying feet, and his own—slower from the longer stride,

121

and the sound of his breath. And for some clear moments he knew that his only concern was to sustain his speed regardless of pain and distress, to deny with every nerve he had her power to outstrip him or to widen the space between them, till the stars crept up to midnight. Then, out again would come that crowd, invisible, humming, and hustling behind, dense and dark enough, he knew, to blot out the stars at his back, yet ever skipping and jerking from his sight.

A hideous check came to the race. White Fell swirled around and leaped to the right, and Christian, unprepared for so prompt a lurch, found close at his feet a deep pit yawning, and his own impetus past control. But he snatched at her as he bore past, clasping her right arm with his one whole hand, and the two swung together upon the brink.

And her straining away in self preservation was vigorous enough to counterbalance his headlong impulse, and brought them reeling together to safety.

Then, before he was verily sure that they were not to perish so, crashing down, he saw her gnashing in wild, pale fury as she wrenched to be free; and since her right hand was in his grasp, used her ax left-handed, striking back at him.

The blow was effectual enough even so; his right arm dropped powerless, gashed, and with the lesser bone broken, that jarred with horrid pain when he let it swing as he leapt out again, and ran to recover the few feet she had gained from his pause at the shock.

The near escape and this new quick pain made again every faculty alive and intense. He knew that what he followed was most surely Death animate: wounded and helpless, he was utterly at her mercy if so she should realize and take action. Hopeless to avenge, hopeless to save, his very despair for Sweyn swept him on to follow, and follow, and precede the kiss doomed to death. Could he yet fail to hunt that Thing past midnight, out of the womanly form alluring and treacherous, into lasting restraint of the bestial, which was the last shred of hope left from the confident purpose of the outset?

"Sweyn, Sweyn, O Sweyn!" He thought he was praying, though his heart wrung out nothing but this: "Sweyn, Sweyn, O Sweyn!"

The last hour from midnight had lost half its quarters, and the stars went lifting up the great minutes; and again his greatening heart, and his shrinking brain, and the sickening agony that swung at either side, conspired to appall the will that had only seeming empire over his feet.

Now, White Fell's body was so closely enveloped that not a lap nor an edge flew free. She stretched forward strangely aslant, leaning from the upright poise of a runner. She cleared the ground at times by long bounds, gaining an increase of speed that Christian agonized to equal.

Because the stars pointed that the end was nearing, the black brood came behind again, and followed, noising. Ah, if they could but be kept quiet and still, nor slip their usual harmless masks to encourage with their interest the last speed of their most deadly congener. What shape had they? Should he ever know? If it were not that he was bound to compel the fell Thing that ran before him into her truer form, he might face about and follow them. No—no—not so; if he might do anything but what he did—race, race, and racing bear this agony, he would just stand still and die, to be quit of the pain of breathing.

He grew bewildered, uncertain of his own identity, doubting of his own true form. He could not be really a man, no more than that running Thing was really a woman; his real form was only hidden under embodiment of a man, but what it was he did not know. And Sweyn's real form he did not know. Sweyn lay fallen at his feet, where he had struck him down—his own brother—he: he stumbled over him, and had to overleaped him and race harder because she who had kissed Sweyn leaped so fast. "Sweyn, Sweyn, O Sweyn!"

Why did the stars stop to shudder? Midnight else had surely come!

The leaning, leaping Thing looked back at him with a wild, fierce look, and laughed in savage scorn and triumph. He saw in a flash why, for within a time measurable by seconds, she would have escaped him utterly. As the land lay, a slope of ice sunk on the one hand; on the other hand, a steep rose, shouldering forward; between the two was space for a foot to be planted, but none for a body to stand; yet a juniper bough, thrusting out, gave a handhold secure enough for one with a resolute grasp to swing past the perilous place, and pass on safe.

Though the first seconds of the last moment were going, she dared to flash back a wicked look, and laugh at the pursuer who was impotent to grasp.

The crisis struck convulsive life into his last supreme effort; his will surged up indomitable, his speed proved matchless yet. He leaped with a rush, passed her before her laugh had time to go out, and turned short, barring the way, and braced to withstand her.

She came hurling, desperate, with a feint to the right hand, and then launched herself upon him with a spring like a wild beast when it leaps to kill. And he, with one strong arm and a hand that could not hold, with one strong hand and an arm that could not guide and sustain, he caught and held her even so. And they fell together. And because he felt his whole arm slipping, and his whole hand loosing, to slack the dreadful agony of the wretched bone above, he caught and held with his teeth the tunic at her knee, as she struggled up and wrung off his hands to overleap him, victorious.

Like lightning, she snatched her ax, and struck him on the neck, deep—once, twice—his lifeblood gushed out, staining her feet.

The stars touched midnight.

The death scream he heard was not his, for his teeth had hardly yet relaxed when it rang out; and the dreadful cry began with a woman's shriek, and changed and ended as the yell of a beast. And before the final blank overtook his dying eyes, he saw that She gave place to It; he saw more, that Life gave place to Death—causelessly, incomprehensibly.

For he did not presume that no holy water could be more

124

holy, more potent to destroy an evil thing than the lifeblood of a pure heart poured out for another in free, willing devotion.

His own true, hidden reality that he had desired to know grew palpable, recognizable. It seemed to him just this: a great, glad, abounding hope that he had saved his brother; too expansive to be contained by the limited form of a sole man, it yearned for a new embodiment infinite as the stars.

What did it matter to that true reality that the man's brain shrank, shrank, till it was nothing; that the man's body could not retain the huge pain of his heart, and heaved it out through the red exit riven at the neck; that the black noise came again hurtling from behind, reinforced by that dissolved shape, and blotted out forever the man's sight, hearing, sense.

# MAMA GONE

*JANE YOLEN*

MAMA DIED FOUR NIGHTS AGO, giving birth to my baby sister Ann. Bubba cried and cried, "Mama gone," in his little-boy voice, but I never let out a single tear.

There was blood red as any sunset all over the bed from that birthing, and when Papa saw it he rubbed his head against the cabin wall over and over and over and made little animal sounds. Sukey washed Mama down and placed the baby on her breast for a moment. "Remember," she whispered.

"Mama gone," Bubba wailed again.

But I never cried.

By all rights, we should have buried her with garlic in her mouth and her hands and feet cut off, what with her being vampire kin and all. But Papa absolutely refused.

"Your Mama couldn't stand garlic," he said when the sounds stopped rushing out of his mouth and his eyes had cleared. "It made her come all over with rashes. She had the sweetest mouth and hands."

And that was that. Not a one of us could make him change his mind, not even Granddad Stokes or Pop Wilber or any other of the men who come to pay their last respects. And as Papa is a preacher, and a brimstone man, they let it be.

126

The onliest thing he would allow was for us to tie red ribbons around her ankles and wrists, a kind of sign like a line of blood. Everybody hoped that would do.

But on the next day, she rose from out her grave and commenced to prey upon the good folk of Taunton.

Of course she came to our house first, that being the dearest place she knew. I saw her outside my window, gray as a gravestone, her dark eyes like the holes in a shroud. When she stared in, she didn't know me, though I had always been her favorite.

"Mama, be gone," I said and waved my little cross at her, the one she had given me the very day I'd been born. "*Avaunt.*" The old Bible word sat heavy in my mouth.

She put her hand up on the window frame, and as I watched, the gray fingers turned splotchy pink from all the garlic I had rubbed into the wood.

Black tears dropped from her black eyes, then. But I never cried.

She tried each window in turn and not a person awake in the house but me. But I had done my work well and the garlic held her out. She even tried the door, but it was no use. By the time she left, I was so sleepy, I dropped down right by the door. Papa found me there at cockcrow. He never did ask what I was doing, and if he guessed, he never said.

Little Joshua Greenough was found dead in his crib. The doctor took two days to come over the mountains to pronounce it. By then, the garlic around his little bed to keep him from walking, too, had mixed with the death smells. Everybody knew. Even the doctor, and him a city man. It hurt his mama and papa sore to do the cutting. But it had to be done.

The men came to our house that very noon to talk about what had to be. Papa kept shaking his head all through their talking. But even his being a preacher didn't stop them. Once a vampire walks these mountain hollars, there's nary a house or barn that's safe. Nighttime is lost time. And no one can afford to lose much stock.

So they made their sharp sticks out of green wood, the curling shavings littering our cabin floor. Bubba played in them, not understanding. Sukey was busy with the baby, nursing it with a bottle and a sugar teat. It was my job to sweep up the wood curls. They felt slick on one side, bumpy on the other. Like my heart.

Papa said, "I was the one let her turn into a night walker. It's my business to stake her out."

No one argued. Specially not the Greenoughs, their eyes still red from weeping.

"Just take my children," Papa said. "And if anything goes wrong, cut off my hands and feet, and bury me at Mill's Cross, under the stone. There's garlic hanging in the pantry. Mandy Jane will string me some."

So Sukey took the baby and Bubba off to the Greenoughs' house, that seeming the right thing to do, and I stayed the rest of the afternoon with Papa, stringing garlic, and pressing more into the windows. But the strand over the door he took down.

"I have to let her in somewhere," he said. "And this is where I'll make my stand." He touched me on the cheek, the first time ever. Papa never has been much for show.

"Now you run along to the Greenoughs', Mandy Jane," he said. "And remember how much your mama loved you. This isn't her, child. Mama's gone. Something else has come to take her place. I should have remembered that the Good Book says, "The living know that they shall die; but the dead know not anything."

I wanted to ask him how the vampire knew to come first to our house, then, but I was silent, for Papa had been asleep and hadn't seen her.

I left without giving him a daughter's kiss, for his mind was well set on the night's doing. But I didn't go down the lane to the Greenoughs' at all. Wearing my triple strand of garlic, with my cross around my neck, I went to the burying ground, to Mama's grave.

It looked so raw against the greening hillside. The dirt was red clay, but all it looked like to me was blood. There was no cross on it yet, no stone. That would come in a year. Just a humping, a heaping of red dirt over her coffin, the plain pinewood box hastily made.

I lay facedown in that dirt, my arms opened wide. "Oh, Mama," I said, "the Good Book says you are not dead but sleepeth. Sleep quietly, Mama, sleep well." And I sang to her the lullaby she had always sung to me and then to Bubba and would have sung to Baby Ann had she lived to hold her.

> *"Blacks and bays,*
> *Dapples and grays,*
> *All the pretty little horses."*

And as I sang I remembered Papa thundering at prayer meeting once, "Behold, a pale horse: and his name that sat on him was Death." The rest of the song just stuck in my throat then, so I turned over on the grave and stared up at the setting sun.

It had been a long and wearying day, and I fell asleep right there in the burying ground. Any other time fear might have overcome sleep. But I just closed my eyes and slept.

When I woke, it was dead night. The moon was full and sitting between the horns of two hills. There was a sprinkling of stars overhead. And Mama began to move the ground beneath me, trying to rise.

The garlic strands must have worried her, for she did not come out of the earth all at once. It was the scrabbling of her long nails at my back that woke me. I leaped off that grave and was wide awake.

Standing aside the grave, I watched as first her long, gray arms reached out of the earth. Then her head, with its hair that was once so gold now gray and streaked with black and its shroud eyes, emerged. And then her body in its winding sheet, stained with dirt, and torn from walking to and fro upon the land. Then her bare feet with blackened nails, though alive Mama used to paint those nails, her one vanity and Papa

129

allowed it seeing she was so pretty, and otherwise not vain.

She turned toward me as a hummingbird toward a flower, and she raised her face up and it was gray and bony. Her mouth peeled back from her teeth, and I saw that they were pointed and her tongue was barbed.

"Mama gone," I whispered in Bubba's voice, but so low I could hardly hear it myself.

She stepped toward me off that grave, lurching down the hump of dirt. But when she got close, the garlic strands and the cross stayed her.

"Mama."

She turned her head back and forth. It was clear she could not see with those black, shroud eyes. She only sensed me there, something warm, something alive, something with the blood running like satisfying streams through the blue veins.

"Mama," I said again. "Try and remember."

That searching awful face turned toward me again, and the pointy teeth were bared once more. Her hands reached out to grab me, then pulled back.

"Remember how Bubba always sucks his thumb with that funny little noise you always said was like a little chuck in its hole. And how Sukey hums through her nose when she's baking bread. And how I listened to your belly to hear the baby. And how Papa always starts each meal with the blessing on things that grow fresh in the field."

The gray face turned for a moment toward the hills, and I wasn't even sure she could hear me. But I had to keep trying.

"And remember when we picked the blueberries and Bubba fell down the hill, tumbling head-end over. And we laughed until we heard him, and he was saying the same six things over and over till long past bed."

The gray face turned back toward me and I thought I saw a bit of light in the eyes. But it was just reflected moonlight.

"And the day Papa came home with the new ewe lamb and we fed her on a sugar teat. You stayed up all the night and I slept in the straw by your side."

It was as if stars were twinkling in those dead eyes.

131

I couldn't stop staring, but I didn't dare stop talking either.

"And remember the day the bluebird stunned itself on the kitchen window, and you held it in your hands. You warmed it to life, you said. To life, Mama."

Those stars began to run down the gray cheeks.

"There's living, Mama, and there's dead. You've given so much life. Don't be bringing death to these hills now." I could see that the stars were gone from the sky over her head; the moon was setting.

"Papa loved you too much to cut your hands and feet. You gotta return that love, Mama. You gotta."

Veins of red ran along the hills, outlining the rocks. As the sun began to rise, I took off one strand of garlic. Then the second. Then the last. I opened my arms. "Have you come back, Mama, or are you gone?"

The gray woman leaned over and clasped me tight in her arms. Her head bent down toward mine, her mouth on my forehead, my neck, the outline of my little gold cross burning across her lips.

She whispered, "Here and gone, child, here and gone," in a voice like wind in the coppice, like the shaking of willow leaves. I felt her kiss on my cheek, a brand.

Then the sun came between the hills and hit her full in the face, burning her as red as earth. She smiled at me and then there was only dust motes in the air, dancing. When I looked down at my feet, the grave dirt was hardly disturbed but Mama's gold wedding band gleamed atop it.

I knelt down and picked it up, and unhooked the chain holding my cross. I slid the ring into the chain, and the two nestled together right in the hollow of my throat.

I sang:

> "Blacks and bays,
> Dapples and grays . . ."

and from the earth itself, the final words sang out,

*"All the pretty little horses."*

That was when I cried, long and loud, a sound I hope never to make again as long as I live.

Then I went back down the hill and home, where Papa still waited by the open door.

# REVELATIONS IN BLACK

*CARL JACOBI*

I T WAS A DREARY, forlorn establishment way down on Harbor Street. An old sign announced the legend: "Giovanni Larla—Antiques," and a dingy window revealed a display half masked in dust.

Even as I crossed the threshold that cheerless September afternoon, driven from the sidewalk by a gust of rain and perhaps a fascination for all antiques, the gloominess fell upon me like a material pall. Inside was half darkness, piled boxes, and a monstrous tapestry, frayed with the warp showing in worn places. An Italian Renaissance wine cabinet shrank despondently in its corner and seemed to frown at me as I passed.

"Good afternoon, *Signor*. There is something you wish to buy? A picture, a ring, a vase perhaps?"

I peered at the squat bulk of the Italian proprietor there in the shadows and hesitated.

"Just looking around," I said, turning to the jumble about me. "Nothing in particular . . . ."

The man's oily face moved in smile as though he had heard the remark a thousand times before. He sighed, stood there in thought a moment, the rain drumming and swishing against

134

the outer pane. Then, very deliberately, he stepped to the shelves and glanced up and down them considering. At length he drew forth an object which I perceived to be a painted chalice.

"An authentic sixteenth-century Tandart," he murmured. "A work of art, *Signor*."

I shook my head. "No pottery," I said. "Books perhaps, but no pottery."

He frowned slowly. "I have books too," he replied, "rare books which nobody sells but me, Giovanni Larla. But you must look at my other treasures too."

There was, I found, no hurrying the man. A quarter of an hour passed during which I had to see a Glycon cameo brooch, a carved chair of some indeterminate style and period, and a muddle of yellowed statuettes, small oils, and one or two dreary Portland vases. Several times I glanced at my watch impatiently, wondering how I might break away from this Italian and his gloomy shop. Already the fascination of its dust and shadows had begun to wear off, and I was anxious to reach the street.

But when he had conducted me well toward the rear of the shop, something caught my fancy. I drew then from the shelf the first book of horror. If I had but known the events that were to follow, if I could only have had a foresight into the future that September day, I swear I would have avoided the book like a leprous thing, would have shunned that wretched antique store and the very street it stood on like places accursed. A thousand times I have wished my eyes had never rested on that cover in black. What writhings of the soul, what terror, what unrest, what madness would have been spared me!

But never dreaming the secret of its pages I fondled it casually and remarked:

"An unusual book. What is it?"

Larla glanced up and scowled.

"That is not for sale," he said quietly. "I don't know how it got on these shelves. It was my poor brother's."

135

The volume in my hand was indeed unusual in appearance. Measuring but four inches across and five inches in length and bound in black velvet with each outside corner protected with a triangle of ivory, it was the most beautiful piece of book-binding I had ever seen. In the center of the cover was mounted a tiny piece of ivory intricately cut in the shape of a skull. But it was the title of the book that excited my interest. Embroidered in gold braid, the title read:

"*Five Unicorns and a Pearl.*"

I looked at Larla. "How much?" I asked and reached for my wallet.

He shook his head. "No, it is not for sale. It is . . . it is the last work of my brother. He wrote it just before he died in the institution."

"The institution?"

Larla made no reply but stood staring at the book, his mind obviously drifting away in deep thought. A moment of silence dragged by. There was a strange gleam in his eyes when finally he spoke. And I thought I saw his fingers tremble slightly.

"My brother, Alessandro, was a fine man before he wrote that book," he said slowly. "He wrote beautifully, *Signor*, and he was strong and healthy. For hours I could sit while he read to me his poems. He was a dreamer, Alessandro; he loved everything beautiful, and the two of us were very happy.

"All . . . until that terrible night. Then he . . . but no . . . a year has passed now. It is best to forget." He passed his hand before his eyes and drew in his breath sharply.

"What happened?" I asked.

"Happened, *Signor*? I do not really know. It was all so confusing. He became suddenly ill, ill without reason. The flush of sunny Italy, which was always on his cheek, faded, and he grew white and drawn. His strength left him day by day. Doctors prescribed, gave medicines, but nothing helped. He grew steadily weaker until . . . until that night."

I looked at him curiously, impressed by his perturbation.

"And then—?"

Hands opening and closing, Larla seemed to sway

unsteadily; his liquid eyes opened wide to the brows.

"And then . . . oh, if I could but forget! It was horrible. Poor Alessandro came home screaming, sobbing. He was . . . he was stark, raving mad!

"They took him to the institution for the insane and said he needed a complete rest, that he had suffered from some terrible mental shock. He . . . died three weeks later with the crucifix on his lips."

For a moment I stood there in silence, staring out at the falling rain. Then I said:

"He wrote this book while confined to the institution?"

Larla nodded absently.

"Three books," he replied. "Two others exactly like the one you have in your hand. The bindings he made, of course, when he was quite well. It was his original intention, I believe, to pen in them by hand the verses of Marini. He was very clever at such work. But the wanderings of his mind which filled the pages now, I have never read. Nor do I intend to. I want to keep with me the memory of him when he was happy. This book has come on these shelves by mistake. I shall put it with his other possessions."

My desire to read the few pages bound in velvet increased a thousand-fold when I found they were unobtainable. I have always had an interest in abnormal psychology and have gone through a number of books on the subject. Here was the work of a man confined in the asylum for the insane. Here was the unexpurgated writing of an educated brain gone mad. And unless my intuition failed me, here was a suggestion of some deep mystery. My mind was made up. I must have it.

I turned to Larla and chose my words carefully.

"I can well appreciate your wish to keep the book," I said, "and since you refuse to sell, may I ask if you would consider lending it to me for just one night? If I promised to return it in the morning? . . . ."

The Italian hesitated. He toyed undecidedly with a heavy, gold watch chain.

"No, I am sorry . . . ."

"Ten dollars and back tomorrow unharmed."

Larla studied his shoe

"Very well, *Signor*, I will trust you. But please, I ask you, please be sure and return it."

That night in the quiet of my apartment I opened the book. Immediately, my attention was drawn to three lines scrawled in a feminine hand across the inside of the front cover, lines written in a faded red solution that looked more like blood than ink. They read:

*"Revelations meant to destroy but only binding without the stake. Read, fool, and enter my field, for we are chained to the spot. Oh woe unto Larla."*

I mused over these undecipherable sentences for some time without solving their meaning. At last, I turned to the first page and began the last work of Alessandro Larla, the strangest story I had ever in my years of browsing through old books, come upon.

*"On the evening of the fifteenth of October I turned my steps into the cold and walked until I was tired. The roar of the present was in the distance when I came to twenty-six bluejays silently contemplating the ruins. Passing in the midst of them, I wandered by the skeleton trees and seated myself where I could watch the leering fish. A child worshiped. Glass threw the moon at me. Grass sang a litany at my feet. And the pointed shadow moved slowly to the left.*

*"I walked along the silver gravel until I came to five unicorns galloping beside water of the past. Here I found a pearl, a magnificent pearl, a pearl beautiful but black. Like a flower, it carried a rich perfume, and once I thought the odor was but a mask, but why should such a perfect creation need a mask?*

*"I sat between the leering fish and the five galloping unicorns, and I fell madly in love with the pearl. The past lost itself in drabness and—"*

I laid the book down and sat watching the smoke-curls from my pipe eddy ceilingward. There was much more, but I could make no sense of any of it. All was in that strange style and completely incomprehensible. And yet it seemed the story was more than the mere wanderings of a madman. Behind it all seemed to lie a narrative cloaked in symbolism.

Something about the few sentences had cast an immediate spell of depression over me. The vague lines weighed upon my mind, and I felt myself slowly seized by a deep feeling of uneasiness.

The air of the room grew heavy and close. The open casement and the out-of-doors seemed to beckon to me. I walked to the window, thrust the curtain aside, stood there, smoking furiously. Let me say that regular habits have long been a part of my makeup. I am not addicted to nocturnal strolls or late meanderings before seeking my bed; yet now, curiously enough, with the pages of the book still in my mind, I suddenly experienced an indefinable urge to leave my apartment and walk the darkened streets.

I paced the room nervously. The clock on the mantel pushed its ticks slowly through the quiet. And at length I threw my pipe to the table, reached for my hat and coat, and made for the door.

Ridiculous as it may sound, upon reaching the street I found that urge had increased to a distinct attraction. I felt that under no circumstances must I turn any direction but northward, and although this way led into a district quite unknown to me, I was in a moment pacing forward, choosing streets deliberately and heading without knowing why toward the outskirts of the city. It was a brilliant moonlit night in September. Summer had passed and already there was the smell of frosted vegetation in the air. The great chimes in Capitol tower were sounding midnight, and the buildings and shops and later the private houses were dark and silent as I passed.

Try as I would to erase from my memory the queer book which I had just read, the mystery of its pages hammered at me, arousing my curiosity. "Five Unicorns and a Pearl!" What did it all mean?

More and more, I realized as I went on that a power other than my own will was leading my steps. Yet, once when I did momentarily come to a halt, that attraction swept upon me as inexorably as the desire for a narcotic.

It was far out on Easterly Street that I came upon a high stone wall flanking the sidewalk. Over its ornamented top I could see the shadows of a dark building set well back in the grounds. A wrought-iron gate in the wall opened upon a view of wild desertion and neglect. Swathed in the light of the moon, an old courtyard strewn with fountains, stone benches and statues lay tangled in rank weeds and undergrowth. The windows of the building, which evidently had once been a private dwelling, were boarded up, all except those on a little tower or cupola rising to a point in front. And here the glass caught the blue-gray light and refracted it into the shadows.

Before that gate my feet stopped like dead things. The psychic power which had been leading me had now become a reality. Directly from the courtyard it emanated, drawing me toward it with an intensity that smothered all reluctance.

Strangely enough, the gate was unlocked; and feeling like a man in a trance, I swung the creaking hinges and entered, making my way along a grass-grown path to one of the benches. It seemed that once inside the court, the distant sounds of the city died away, leaving a hollow silence broken only by the wind rustling through the tall, dead weeds. Rearing up before me, the building with its dark wings, cupola and façade oddly resembled a colossal hound, crouched and ready to spring.

There were several fountains, weather-beaten and ornamented with curious figures, to which at the time I paid only casual attention. Farther on, half hidden by the underbrush, was the life-size statue of a little child kneeling in a position of prayer. Erosion on the soft stone had disfigured the face, and in the half-light the carved features presented an expression strangely grotesque and repelling.

How long I sat there in the quiet, I don't know. The surroundings under the moonlight blended harmoniously with my mood. But more than that, I seemed physically unable to rouse myself and pass on.

It was with a suddenness that brought me electrified to my feet that I became aware of the significance of the objects around me. Held motionless, I stood there running my eyes wildly from place to place, refusing to believe. Surely I must be dreaming. In the name of all that was unusual this . . . this absolutely couldn't be. And yet—

It was the fountain at my side that had caught my attention first. Across the top of the water basin were *five stone unicorns*, all identically carved, each seeming to follow the other in galloping procession. Looking farther, prompted now by a madly rising recollection, I saw that the cupola, towering high above the house, eclipsed the rays of the moon and threw a *long pointed shadow* across the ground *at my left*. The other fountain some distance away was ornamented with the figure of a stone fish, *a fish* whose empty eye-sockets *were leering* straight in my direction. And the climax of it all—the wall! At intervals of every three feet on the top of the street expanse were mounted crude, carven stone shapes of birds. And counting them I saw that *those birds were twenty-six bluejays*.

Unquestionably—startling and impossible as it seemed—I was in the same setting as described in Larla's book! It was a staggering revelation, and my mind reeled at the thought of it. How strange, how odd that I should be drawn to a portion of the city I had never before frequented and thrown into the midst of a narrative written almost a year before!

I saw now that Alessandro Larla, writing as a patient in the institution for the insane, had seized isolated details but neglected to explain them. Here was a problem for the psychologist, the mad, the symbolic, the incredible story of the dead Italian. I was bewildered and I pondered for an answer.

As if to soothe my perturbation, there stole into the court then a faint odor of perfume. Pleasantly, it touched my nostrils, seemed to blend with the moonlight. I breathed it in deeply as I stood there by the fountain. But slowly that odor became more noticeable, grew stronger, a sickish sweet smell that began to creep down my lungs like smoke. Heliotrope!

The honeyed aroma blanketed the garden, thickened the air.

And then came my second surprise of the evening. Looking around to discover the source of the fragrance, I saw opposite me, seated on another stone bench, a woman. She was dressed entirely in black, and her face was hidden by a veil. She seemed unaware of my presence. Her head was slightly bowed, and her whole position suggested a person in deep contemplation.

I noticed also the thing that crouched by her side. It was a dog, a tremendous brute with a head strangely out of proportion, and eyes as large as the ends of big spoons. For several moments I stood staring at the two of them. Although the air was quite chilly, the woman wore no overcoat, only the black dress relieved solely by the whiteness of her throat.

With a sigh of regret at having my pleasant solitude thus disturbed, I moved across the court until I stood at her side. Still she showed no recognition of my presence, and clearing my throat I said hesitatingly:

"I suppose you are the owner here. I . . . I really didn't know the place was occupied, and the gate . . . well, the gate was unlocked. I'm sorry I trespassed."

She made no reply to that, and the dog merely gazed at me in dumb silence. No graceful words of polite departure came to my lips, and I moved hesitatingly toward the gate.

"Please don't go," she said suddenly, looking up. "I'm lonely. Oh, if you but knew how lonely I am!" She moved to one side on the bench and motioned that I sit beside her. The dog continued to examine me with its big eyes.

Whether it was the nearness of that odor of heliotrope, the suddenness of it all, or perhaps the moonlight, I did not know, but at her words a thrill of pleasure ran through me, and I accepted the proffered seat.

There followed an interval of silence, during which I puzzled for a means to start conversation. But abruptly she turned to the beast and said in German:

"*Fort mit dir, Johann!*"

The dog rose obediently to its feet and stole slowly off into

the shadows. I watched it for a moment until it disappeared in the direction of the house. Then the woman said to me in English which was slightly stilted and marked with an accent:

"It has been ages since I have spoken to anyone . . . We are strangers. I do not know you, and you do not know me. Yet . . . strangers sometimes find in each other a bond of interest. Supposing . . . supposing we forget customs and formality of introduction? Shall we?"

For some reason I felt my pulse quicken as she said that. "Please do," I replied. "A spot like this is enough introduction in itself. Tell me, do you live here?"

She made no answer for a moment, and I began to fear I had taken her suggestion too quickly. Then she began slowly:

"My name is Perle von Mauren, and I am really a stranger to your country, though I have been here now more than a year. My home is in Austria, near what is now the Czechoslovakian frontier. You see, it was to find my only brother that I came to the United States. During the war, he was a lieutenant under General Mackensen, but in 1916, in April I believe it was, he . . . he was reported missing.

"War is a cruel thing. It took our money, it took our castle on the Danube, and then—my brother. Those following years were horrible. We lived always in doubt, hoping against hope that he was still living.

"Then, after the Armistice, a fellow officer claimed to have served next to him on grave-digging detail at a French prison camp near Monpré. And later came a thin rumor that he was in the United States. I gathered together as much money as I could and came here in search of him."

Her voice dwindled off, and she sat in silence staring at the brown weeds. When she resumed, her voice was low and wavering.

"I . . . found him . . . but would to God I hadn't! He . . . he was no longer living."

I stared at her. "Dead?" I asked.

The veil trembled as though moved by a shudder, as though her thoughts had exhumed some terrible event of the past. Unconscious of my interruption, she went on:

"Tonight I came here—I don't know why—merely because the gate was unlocked, and there was a place of quiet within. Now have I bored you with my confidences and personal history?"

"Not at all," I replied. "I came here by chance myself. Probably the beauty of the place attracted me. I dabble in amateur photography occasionally and react strongly to unusual scenes. Tonight I went for a midnight stroll to relieve my mind from the bad effect of a book I was reading."

She made a strange reply to that, a reply away from our line of thought and which seemed an interjection that escaped her involuntarily.

"Books," she said, "are powerful things. They can fetter one more than the walls of a prison."

She caught my puzzled stare at the remark and added hastily: "It is odd that we should meet here."

For a moment, I didn't answer. I was thinking of her heliotrope perfume, which for a woman of her apparent culture was applied in far too great a quantity to show good taste. The impression stole upon me that the perfume cloaked some secret, that if it were removed I should find . . . but what?

The hours passed, and still we sat there talking, enjoying each other's companionship. She did not remove her veil, and though I was burning with desire to see her features, I had not dared to ask her to. A strange nervousness had slowly seized me. The woman was a charming conversationalist, but there was about her an indefinable something which produced in me a distinct feeling of unease.

It was, I should judge, but a few moments before the first streaks of a dawn when it happened. As I look back now, even with mundane objects and thoughts on every side, it is not difficult to realize the significance of that vision. But, at the time, my brain was too much in a whirl to understand.

A thin shadow moving across the garden attracted my gaze once again into the night around me. I looked up over the spire of the deserted house and started, as if struck by a blow. For a moment, I thought I had seen a curious cloud formation racing low directly above me, a cloud black and impenetrable with two winglike ends strangely in the shape of a monstrous flying bat.

I blinked my eyes hard and looked again.

"That cloud!" I exclaimed. "That strange cloud! . . . Did you see—"

I stopped and stared dumbly.

The bench at my side was empty. The woman had disappeared.

During the next day I went about my professional duties in the law office with only half interest, and my business partner looked at me queerly several times when he came upon me mumbling to myself. The incidents of the evening before were rushing through my mind. Questions unanswerable hammered at me. That I should have come upon the very details described by mad Larla in his strange book: the leering fish, the praying child, the twenty-six bluejays, the pointed shadow of the cupola—it was unexplainable; it was weird.

"Five Unicorns and a Pearl." The unicorns were the stone statues ornamenting the old fountain, yes—but the pearl? With a start I suddenly recalled the name of the woman in black: Perle von Mauren. What did it all mean?

Dinner had little attraction for me that evening. Earlier, I had gone to the antique-dealer and begged him to loan me the sequel, the second volume of his brother Alessandro. When he had refused, objected because I had not yet returned the first book, my nerves had suddenly jumped on edge. I felt like a narcotic fiend faced with the realizations that he could not procure the desired drug. In desperation, yet hardly knowing why, I offered the man more money, until at length I had come away, my powers of persuasion and my pocketbook successful.

The second volume was identical in outward respects to its predecessor except that it bore no title. But if I was expecting more disclosures in symbolism I was doomed to disappointment. Vague as "Five Unicorns and a Pearl" had been, the text of the sequel was even more wandering and was obviously only the ramblings of a mad brain. By watching the sentences closely, I did gather that Alessandro Larla had made a second trip to his court of the twenty-six bluejays and met there again his "pearl."

There was the paragraph toward the end that puzzled me. It read:

*"Can it possibly be? I pray that it is not. And yet I have seen it and heard it snarl. Oh, the loathsome creature! I will not, I will not believe it."*

I closed the book and tried to divert my attention elsewhere by polishing the lens of my newest portable camera. But again, as before, that same urge stole upon me, that same desire to visit the garden. I confess that I had watched the intervening hours until I would meet the woman in black again; for strangely enough, in spite of her abrupt exit before, I never doubted that she would be there waiting for me. I wanted her to lift the veil. I wanted to talk with her. I wanted to throw myself once again into the narrative of Larla's book.

Yet the whole thing seemed preposterous, and I fought the sensation with every ounce of willpower I could call to mind. Then it suddenly occurred to me what a remarkable picture she would make, sitting there on the stone bench, clothed in black, with the classic background of the old courtyard. If I could but catch the scene on a photographic plate . . . .

I halted my polishing and mused a moment. With a new electric flash lamp, that handy invention which has supplanted the old mussy flash powder, I could illuminate the garden and snap the picture with ease. And if the result were satisfactory, it would make a worthy contribution to the International Camera Contest at Geneva next month.

The idea appealed to me, and gathering together the necessary equipment, I drew on a coat (for it was a wet, chilly night) and slipped out of my rooms and headed northward. Mad, unseeing fool that I was! If only I had stopped then and there, returned the book to the antique dealer, and closed the incident! But the strange magnetic attraction had gripped me in earnest, and I rushed headlong into the horror.

A fall rain was drumming the pavement, and the streets were deserted. Off to the east, however, the heavy blanket of clouds glowed with a soft radiance where the moon was trying to break through, and a strong wind from the south gave promise of clearing the skies before long. With my coat collar turned well up at the throat, I passed once again into the older section of the town and down forgotten Easterly Street. I found the gate to the grounds unlocked as before, and the garden a dripping place masked in shadow.

The woman was not there. Still the hour was early, and I did not for a moment doubt that she would appear later. Gripped now with the enthusiasm of my plan, I set the camera carefully on the stone fountain, training the lens as well as I could on the bench where we had sat the previous evening. The flash lamp with its battery handle I laid within reach.

Scarcely had I finished my arrangements when the crunch of gravel on the path caused me to turn. She was approaching the stone bench, heavily veiled as before, and with the same sweeping black dress.

"You have come again," she said as I took my place beside her.

"Yes," I replied. "I could not stay away."

Our conversation that night gradually centered around her dead brother, although I thought several times that the woman tried to avoid the subject. He had been, it seemed, the black sheep of the family, had led more or less of a dissolute life, and had been expelled from the University of Vienna not only because of his lack of respect for the pedagogues of the various sciences but also because of his queer, unorthodox papers on philosophy. His sufferings in the war prison camp must have been intense. With a kind of grim delight, she dwelt on his horrible experiences in the grave-digging detail which had been related to her by the fellow officer. But of the manner in which he had met his death, she would say absolutely nothing.

Stronger than on the night before was the sweet smell of heliotrope. And again, as the fumes crept nauseatingly down my lungs, there came that same sense of nervousness, that same feeling that the perfume was hiding something I should know. The desire to see beneath the veil had become maddening by this time, but still I lacked the boldness to ask her to lift it.

Toward midnight the heavens cleared and the moon in splendid contrast shone high in the sky. The time had come for my picture.

"Sit where you are," I said. "I'll be back in a moment."

Stepping to the fountain I grasped the flash lamp, held it aloft for an instant, and placed my finger on the shutter lever of the camera. The woman remained motionless on the bench, evidently puzzled as to the meaning of my movements. The range was perfect. A click, and a dazzling white light enveloped the courtyard around us. For a brief second she was outlined there against the old wall. Then the blue moonlight returned, and I was smiling in satisfaction.

"It ought to make a beautiful picture," I said.

She leaped to her feet.

"Fool!" she cried hoarsely. "Blundering fool! What have you done?"

Even though the veil was there to hide her face, I got the instant impression that her eyes were glaring at me, smoldering with hatred. I gazed at her curiously as she stood erect, head thrown back, body apparently taut as wire, and a slow shudder crept down my spine. Then, without warning, she gathered up her dress and ran down the path toward the deserted house. A moment later, she had disappeared somewhere in the shadows of the giant bushes.

I stood there by the fountain, staring after her in a daze. Suddenly, off in the umbra of the house's façade, there rose a low animal snarl.

And then, before I could move, a huge gray shape came hurtling through the long woods, bounding in great leaps straight toward me. It was the woman's dog, which I had seen

149

with her the night before. But no longer was it a beast passive and silent. Its face was contorted in diabolic fury, and its jaws were dripping saliva. Even in that moment of terror as I stood frozen before it, the sight of those white nostrils and those black hyalescent eyes emblazoned itself on my mind, never to be forgotten.

Then with a lunge it was upon me. I had only time to thrust the flash lamp upward in half protection and throw my weight to the side. My arm jumped in recoil. The bulb exploded, and I could feel those teeth clamp down hard on the handle. Backward I fell, a scream gurgling to my lips, a terrific heaviness surging upon my body.

I struck out frantically, beat my fists into that growling face. My fingers groped blindly for its throat, sank deep into the hairy flesh. I could feel its very breath mingling with my own now, but desperately I hung on.

The pressure of my hands told. The dog coughed and fell back. And, seizing that instant, I struggled to my feet, jumped forward and planted a terrific kick straight into the brute's middle.

"*Fort mit dir, Johann!*" I cried, remembering the woman's German command.

It leaped back and, fangs bared, glared at me motionless for a moment. Then abruptly it turned, and slunk off through the weeds.

Weak and trembling, I drew myself together, picked up my camera, and passed through the gate toward home.

Three days passed. Those endless hours I spent confined to my apartment suffering the tortures of the damned.

On the day following the night of my terrible experience with the dog, I realized I was in no condition to go to work. I drank two cups of strong black coffee and then forced myself to sit quietly in a chair, hoping to soothe my nerves. But the sight of the camera there on the table excited me to action. Five minutes later I was in the dark room arranged as my studio, developing the picture I had taken the night before. I worked feverishly, urged on by the thought of what an unusual contribution it would make for the amateur contest next month at Geneva, should the result be successful.

An exclamation burst from my lips as I stared at the still-wet print. There was the old garden clear and sharp with the bushes, the statue of the child, the fountain and the wall in the background, but the bench—the stone bench was empty. There was no sign, not even a blur of the woman in black.

I rushed the negative through a saturated solution of mercuric chloride in water, then treated it with ferrous oxalate. But even after this intensifying process, the second print was like the first, focused in every detail, the bench standing in the foreground in sharp relief, but no trace of the woman.

She had been in plain view when I snapped the shutter. Of that I was positive. And my camera was in perfect condition. What then was wrong? Not until I had looked at the print hard in the daylight would I believe my eyes. No explanation offered itself, none at all; and at length, confused, I returned to my bed and fell into a heavy sleep.

Straight through the day I slept. Hours later, I seemed to wake from a vague nightmare, and had not strength to rise from my pillow. A great physical faintness had overwhelmed me. My arms, my legs, lay like dead things. My heart was fluttering weakly. All was quiet, so still that the clock on my bureau ticked distinctly each passing second. The curtain billowed in the night breeze, though I was positive I had closed the casement when I entered the room.

And then suddenly, I threw back my head and screamed! For slowly, slowly, creeping down my lungs was that detestable odor of heliotrope!

Morning, and I found all was not a dream. My head was ringing, my hands trembling, and I was so weak I could hardly stand. The doctor I called in looked grave as he felt my pulse.

"You are on the verge of a complete collapse," he said. "If you do not allow yourself a rest it may permanently affect your mind. Take things easy for a while. And if you don't mind, I'll cauterize those two little cuts on your neck. They're rather raw wounds. What caused them?"

I moved my fingers to my throat and drew them away again tipped with blood.

"I . . . I don't know," I faltered.

He busied himself with his medicines, and a few minutes later reached for his hat.

"I advise that you don't leave your bed for a week at least," he said. "I'll give you a thorough examination then and see if there are any signs of anemia." But as he went out the door, I thought I saw a puzzled look on his face.

Those subsequent hours allowed my thoughts to run wild once more. I vowed I would forget it all, go back to my work, and never look upon the books again. But I knew I could not. The woman in black persisted in my mind, and each minute away from her became a torture. But more than that, if there had been a decided urge to continue my reading in the second book, the desire to see the third book, the last of the trilogy, was slowly increasing to an obsession.

At length I could stand it no longer, and on the morning of the third day I took a cab to the antique shop and tried to persuade Larla to give me the third volume by his brother. But the Italian was firm. I had already taken two books, neither of which I had returned. Until I brought them back, he would not listen. Vainly I tried to explain that one was of no value without the sequel, and that I wanted to read the entire narrative as a unit. He merely shrugged his shoulders.

Cold perspiration broke out on my forehead as I heard my desire disregarded. I argued. I pleaded. But to no avail.

At length, when Larla had turned the other way, I seized the third book as I saw it lying on the shelf, slid it into my pocket and walked guiltily out. I made no apologies for my action. In the light of what developed later, it may be considered a temptation inspired, for my will at the time was a conquered thing blanketed by that strange lure.

Back in my apartment, I dropped into a chair and hastened to open the velvet cover. Here was the last chronicling of that strange series of events which had so completely become a part of my life during the past five days. Larla's volume three. Would all be explained in its pages? If so, what secret would be revealed?

With the light from a reading lamp glaring full over my shoulder, I opened the book, thumbed through it slowly, marveling again at the exquisite hand-printing. It seemed then as I sat there that an almost palpable cloud of quiet settled over me, muffling the distant sounds of the street. Something indefinable seemed to forbid me to read further. Curiosity, that queer urge, told me to go on. Slowly, I began to turn the pages, one at a time, from back to front.

Symbolism again. Vague wanderings, with no sane meaning.

But suddenly, my fingers stopped! My eyes had caught sight of the last paragraph on the last page, the final pennings of Alessandro Larla. I read, re-read, and read again those blasphemous words. I traced each word in the lamplight, slowly, carefully, letter for letter. Then the horror of it burst within me.

In blood-red ink the lines read:

*"What shall I do? She has drained my blood and rotted my soul. My pearl is black as all evil. The curse be upon her brother, for it is he who made her thus. I pray the truth in these pages will destroy them forever.*

*"Heaven help me, Perle von Mauren and her brother, Johann, are vampires!"*

I leaped to my feet.

"Vampires!"

I clutched at the edge of the table and stood there swaying. Vampires! Those horrible creatures with a lust for human blood, taking the shape of men, of bats, of dogs.

The events of the past days rose before me in all their horror now, and I could see the black significance of every detail.

The brother, Johann—sometime since the war—he had become a vampire. When the woman sought him out years later, he had forced this terrible existence upon her too.

With the garden as their lair, the two of them had entangled poor Alessandro Larla in their serpentine coils a year before. He had loved the woman, had worshiped her. And then he had found the awful truth that had sent him stumbling home, raving mad.

Mad, yes, but not mad enough to keep him from writing the fact in his three velvet-bound books. He had hoped the disclosures would dispatch the woman and her brother forever. But it was not enough.

I whipped the first book from the table and opened the cover. There again I saw those scrawled lines which had meant nothing to me before.

*"Revelations meant to destroy but only binding without the stake. Read, fool, and enter my field, for we are chained to the spot. Oh, woe unto Larla!"*

Perle von Mauren had written that. The books had not put an end to the evil life of her and her brother. No, only one thing could do that. Yet the exposures had not been written in vain. They were recorded for mortal posterity to see.

Those books bound the two vampires, Perle von Mauren, Johann, to the old garden, kept them from roaming the night streets in search of victims. Only he who had once passed through the gate could they pursue and attack.

It was the old metaphysical law: evil shrinking in the face of truth.

Yet, if the books had found their power in chains, they had also opened a new avenue for their attacks. Once immersed in the pages of the trilogy, the reader fell helplessly into their clutches. Those printed lines had become the outer reaches of their web. They were an entrapping net within which the power of the vampires always crouched.

That was why my life had blended so strangely with the story of Larla. The moment I had cast my eyes on the opening paragraph, I had fallen into their coils to do with as they had done with Larla a year before. I had been drawn relentlessly into the tentacles of the woman in black. Once I was past the garden gate, the binding spell of the books was gone, and they were free to pursue me and to—

A giddy sensation rose within me. Now I saw why the doctor had been puzzled. Now I saw the reason for my physical weakness. She had been—feasting on my blood! But if Larla had been ignorant of the one way to dispose of such a creature, I was not. I had not vacationed in southern Europe without learning something of these ancient evils.

Frantically, I looked around the room. A chair, a table, one of my cameras with its long tripod. I seized one of the wooden legs of the tripod in my hands, snapped it across my knee. Then, grasping the two broken pieces, both now with sharp splintered ends, I rushed hatless out of the door to the street.

A moment later I was racing northward in a cab bound for Easterly Street.

"Hurry!" I cried to the driver as I glanced at the westering sun. "Faster, do you hear?"

We shot along the cross-streets, into the old suburbs, and toward the outskirts of town. Every traffic halt found me fuming at the delay. But at length we drew up before the wall of the garden.

I swung the wrought-iron gate open and, with the wooden pieces of the tripod still under my arm, rushed in. The courtyard was a place of reality in the daylight, but the moldering masonry and tangled weeds were steeped in silence as before.

Straight for the house I made, climbing the rotten steps to the front entrance. The door was boarded up and locked. I retraced my steps and began to circle the south wall of the building. It was this direction I had seen the woman take when she had fled after I had tried to snap her picture. Well toward the rear of the building, I reached a small half-open door leading to the cellar. Inside, cloaked in gloom, a narrow corridor stretched before me. The floor was littered with rubble and fallen masonry, the ceiling interlaced with a thousand cobwebs.

I stumbled forward, my eyes quickly accustoming themselves to the half-light from the almost opaque windows.

At the end of the corridor a second door barred my passage. I thrust it open—and stood swaying there on the sill staring inward.

Beyond was a small room, barely ten-feet square, with a low-raftered ceiling. And by the light of the open door, I saw side by side in the center of the floor—two white wood coffins.

How long I stood there leaning weakly against the stone wall I don't know. There was an odor drifting from out of that chamber. Heliotrope! But heliotrope defiled by the rotting smell of an ancient grave.

Then suddenly, I leaped to the nearest coffin, seized its cover, and ripped it open.

Would to heaven I could forget that sight that met my eyes. There lay the woman in black—unveiled.

That face—it was divinely beautiful, the hair black as sable, the cheeks a classic white. But the lips—! I grew suddenly sick as I looked upon them. They were scarlet . . . and sticky with human blood.

I reached for one of the tripod stakes, seized a flagstone from the floor and, with the pointed end of the wood resting directly over the woman's heart, struck a crashing blow. The stake jumped downward. A violent contortion shook the coffin. Up to my face rushed a warm, nauseating breath of decay.

I wheeled and hurled open the lid of her brother's coffin. With only a glance at the young masculine Teutonic face, I raised the other stake high in the air and brought it stabbing down with all the strength in my right arm.

In the coffin now, staring up at me from eyeless sockets, were two gray and moldering skeletons.

The rest is but a vague dream. I remember rushing outside, along the path to the gate and down Easterly, away from that accursed garden of the jays.

At length, utterly exhausted, I reached my apartment. Those mundane surroundings that confronted me were like balm to my eyes. But there, centered into my gaze, three objects lying where I had left them, the three volumes of Larla.

I turned to the grate on the other side of the room and flung the three of them on to the still glowing coals.

There was an instant hiss, and yellow flame streaked upward and began eating into the velvet. The fire grew higher . . . higher . . . and diminished slowly.

And as the last glowing spark died into a blackened ash, there swept over me a mighty feeling of quiet and relief.

# GABRIEL-ERNEST

### SAKI (H. H. MUNRO)

"THERE IS A WILD BEAST in your woods," said the artist Cunningham, as he was being driven to the station. It was the only remark he had made during the drive, but as Van Cheele had talked incessantly, his companion's silence had not been noticeable.

"A stray fox or two and some resident weasels. Nothing more formidable," said Van Cheele. The artist said nothing.

"What did you mean about a wild beast?" said Van Cheele later, when they were on the platform.

"Nothing. My imagination. Here is the train," said Cunningham.

That afternoon, Van Cheele went for one of his frequent rambles through his woodland property. He had a stuffed heron in his study, and knew the names of quite a number of wild flowers, so his aunt had possibly some justification in describing him as a great naturalist. At any rate, he was a great walker. It was his custom to take mental notes of everything he saw during his walks, not so much for the purpose of assisting contemporary science as to provide topics for conversation afterward. When the bluebells began to show themselves in flower, he made a point of informing everyone of the fact; the season of the year might have warned his hearers of the likelihood of such an occurrence, but at least they felt that he was being absolutely frank with them.

What Van Cheele saw on this particular afternoon was, however, something far removed from his ordinary range of experience. On a shelf of smooth stone overhanging a deep pool in the hollow of an oak coppice a boy of about sixteen lay asprawl, drying his wet brown limbs luxuriously in the sun. His wet hair, parted by a recent dive, lay close to his head, and his light-brown eyes, so light that there was an almost tigerish gleam in them, were turned toward Van Cheele with a certain lazy watchfulness. It was an unexpected apparition, and Van Cheele found himself engaged in the novel process of thinking before he spoke. Where on earth could this wild-looking boy hail from? The miller's wife had lost a child some two months ago, supposed to have been swept away by the millstream, but that had been a mere baby, not a half-grown lad.

"What are you doing there?" he demanded.

"Obviously, sunning myself," replied the boy.

"Where do you live?"

"Here, in these woods."

"You can't live in the woods," said Van Cheele.

"They are very nice woods," said the boy, with a touch of patronage in his voice.

"But where do you sleep at night?"

"I don't sleep at night; that's my busiest time."

Van Cheele began to have an irritated feeling that he was grappling with a problem that was eluding him.

"What do you feed on?" he asked.

"Flesh," said the boy, and he pronounced the word with slow relish, as though he were tasting it.

"Flesh! What flesh?"

"Since it interests you, rabbits, wildfowl, hares, poultry, lambs in their season, and children when I can get any; they're usually too well locked-in at night, when I do most of my hunting. It's quite two months since I tasted child-flesh."

Ignoring the chaffing nature of the last remark, Van Cheele

tried to draw the boy on the subject of possible poaching operations.

"You're talking rather through your hat when you speak of feeding on hares." (Considering the nature of the boy's toilet, the simile was hardly an apt one.) "Our hillside hares aren't easily caught."

"At night, I hunt on four feet," was the somewhat cryptic response.

"I suppose you mean that you hunt with a dog?" hazarded Van Cheele.

The boy rolled slowly over onto his back, and laughed a weird, low laugh that was pleasantly like a chuckle, and disagreeably like a snarl.

"I don't fancy any dog would be very anxious for my company, especially at night."

Van Cheele began to feel that there was something positively uncanny about the strange-eyed, strange-tongued youngster.

"I can't have you staying in these woods," he declared authoritatively.

"I fancy you'd rather have me here than in your house," said the boy.

The prospect of this wild, nude animal in Van Cheele's primly-ordered house was certainly an alarming one.

"If you don't go, I shall have to make you," said Van Cheele.

The boy turned like a flash, plunged into the pool, and in a moment had flung his wet and glistening body halfway up the bank where Van Cheele was standing. In an otter, the movement would not have been remarkable; in a boy, Van Cheele found it sufficiently startling. His foot slipped as he made an involuntary backward movement, and he found himself almost prostrate on the slippery weed-grown bank, with those tigerish, yellow eyes not very far from his own. Almost instinctively, he half-raised his hand to his throat. The boy laughed again, a laugh in which the snarl had nearly driven out the chuckle, and then, with another of his astonishing, lightning movements, plunged out of view into a yielding tangle of weed and fern.

"What an extraordinary wild animal!" said Van Cheele as he picked himself up. And then he recalled Cunningham's remark, "There is a wild beast in your woods."

Walking-slowly homeward, Van Cheele began to turn over in his mind various local occurrences which might be traceable to the existence of this astonishing young savage.

Something had been thinning the game in the woods lately, poultry had been missing from the farms, hares were growing unaccountably scarcer, and complaints had reached him of lambs being carried off bodily from the hills. Was it possible that this wild boy was really hunting the countryside in company with some clever poacher dog? He had spoken of hunting "four-footed" by night, but then, again, he had hinted strangely at no dog caring to come near him, "especially at night." It was certainly puzzling. And then, as Van Cheele ran his mind over the various depredations that had been committed during the last month or two, he came suddenly to a dead stop, alike in his walk and his speculations. The child missing from the mill two months ago—the accepted theory was that it had tumbled into the millrace and been swept away, but the mother had always declared she had heard a shriek on the hill side of the house, in the opposite direction from the water. It was unthinkable, of course, but he wished that the boy had not made that uncanny remark about child-flesh eaten two months ago. Such dreadful things should not be said, even in fun.

Van Cheele, contrary to his usual wont, did not feel disposed to be communicative about his discovery in the wood. His position as a parish councillor and justice of the peace seemed somehow compromised by the fact that he was harboring a personality of such doubtful repute on his property, there was even a possibility that a heavy bill for damages for raided lambs and poultry might be laid at his door. At dinner that night he was quite unusually silent.

"Where's your voice gone to?" said his aunt. "One would think you had seen a wolf."

Van Cheele, who was not familiar with the old saying, thought the remark rather foolish; if he *had* seen a wolf on his property, his tongue would have been extraordinarily busy with the subject.

At breakfast next morning, Van Cheele was conscious that his feeling of uneasiness regarding yesterday's episode had not wholly disappeared, and he resolved to go by train to the neighboring cathedral town, hunt up Cunningham, and learn from him what he had really seen that had prompted the remark about a wild beast in the woods. With this resolution taken, his usual cheerfulness partially returned, and he hummed a bright little melody as he sauntered to the morning room for his customary cigarette. As he entered the room, the melody made way abruptly for a pious invocation. Gracefully asprawl on the ottoman, in an attitude of almost exaggerated repose, was the boy of the woods. He was drier than when Van Cheele had last seen him, but no other alteration was noticeable in his appearance.

"How dare you come here?" asked Van Cheele furiously.

"You told me I was not to stay in the woods," said the boy calmly.

"But not to come here. Supposing my aunt should see you!"

And with a view to minimizing that catastrophe, Van Cheele hastily obscured as much of his unwelcome guest as possible under the folds of a *Morning Post*. At that moment, his aunt entered the room.

"This is a poor boy who has lost his way—and lost his memory. He doesn't know who he is or where he comes from," explained Van Cheele desperately, glancing apprehensively at the waif's face to see whether he was going to add inconvenient candor to his other savage propensities.

Miss Van Cheele was enormously interested.

"Perhaps his underlinen is marked," she suggested.

"He seems to have lost most of that, too," said Van Cheele, making frantic little grabs at the *Morning Post* to keep it in its place.

A naked, homeless child appealed to Miss Van Cheele as warmly as a stray kitten or derelict puppy would have done.

"We must do all we can for him," she decided, and in a very short time a messenger, dispatched to the rectory, where a page-boy was kept, had returned with a suit of pantry clothes, and the necessary accessories of shirt, shoes, collar, etc. Clothed, clean, and groomed, the boy lost none of his uncanniness in Van Cheele's eyes, but his aunt found him sweet.

"We must call him something till we know who he really is," she said. "Gabriel-Ernest, I think; those are nice, suitable names."

Van Cheele agreed, but he privately doubted whether they were being grafted on to a nice, suitable child. His misgivings were not diminished by the fact that his staid and elderly spaniel had bolted out of the house at the first incoming of the boy, and now obstinately remained shivering and yapping at the farther end of the orchard, while the canary, usually as vocally industrious as Van Cheele himself, had put itself on an allowance of frightened cheeps. More than ever, he was resolved to consult Cunningham without loss of time.

As he drove off to the station, his aunt was arranging that Gabriel-Ernest should help her to entertain the infant members of her Sunday-school class at tea that afternoon.

Cunningham was not at first disposed to be communicative.

"My mother died of some brain trouble," he explained, "so you will understand why I am averse to dwelling on anything of an impossibly fantastic nature that I may see or think that I have seen."

"But what did you see?" persisted Van Cheele.

"What I thought I saw was something so extraordinary that no really sane man could dignify it with the credit of having actually happened. I was standing, the last evening I was with you, half-hidden in the hedge growth by the orchard gate, watching the dying glow of the sunset. Suddenly, I became aware of a naked boy, a bather from some neighboring pool, I took him to be, who was standing out on the bare hillside also watching the sunset. His pose was so suggestive of some wild faun of Pagan myth that I instantly wanted to engage him as a model, and in another moment I think I should have hailed him. But just then the sun dipped out of view, and all the orange and pink slid out of the landscape, leaving it cold and gray. And at the same moment, an astounding thing happened—the boy vanished too!"

"What! Vanished away into nothing?" asked Van Cheele excitedly.

"No; that is the dreadful part of it," answered the artist; "on the open hillside where the boy had been standing a second ago, stood a large wolf, blackish in color, with gleaming fangs and cruel, yellow eyes. You may think—"

But Van Cheele did not stop for anything as futile as thought. Already he was tearing at top speed towards the station. He dismissed the idea of a telegram. "Gabriel-Ernest is a werewolf" was a hopelessly inadequate effort at conveying the situation, and his aunt would think it was a code message to which he had omitted to give her the key. His one hope was that he might reach home before sundown. The cab which he chartered at the other end of the railway journey bore him with what seemed exasperating slowness along the country roads, which were pink and mauve with the flush of the sinking sun. His aunt was putting away some unfinished jams and cake when he arrived.

"Where is Gabriel-Ernest?" he almost screamed.

"He is taking the little Toop child home," said his aunt. "It was getting so late, I thought it wasn't safe to let it go back alone. What a lovely sunset, isn't it?"

But Van Cheele, although not oblivious to the glow in the western sky, did not stay to discuss its beauties. At a speed for which he was scarcely geared, he raced along the narrow lane that led to the home of the Toops. On one side ran the swift current of the mill-stream, on the other rose the stretch of bare hillside. A dwindling rim of red sun showed still on the skyline, and the next turning must bring him in view of the ill-assorted couple he was pursuing. Then the color went suddenly out of things, and a gray light settled itself with a

quick shiver over the landscape. Van Cheele heard a shrill wail of fear, and stopped running.

Nothing was ever seen again of the Toop child or Gabriel-Ernest, but the latter's discarded garments were found lying in the road, so it was assumed that the child had fallen into the water, and that the boy had stripped and jumped in, in a vain endeavor to save it. Van Cheele and some workmen who were near by at the time testified to having heard a child scream loudly just near the spot where the clothes were found. Mrs. Toop, who had eleven other children, was decently resigned to her bereavement, but Miss Van Cheele sincerely mourned her lost foundling. It was on her initiative that a memorial brass was put up in the parish church to "Gabriel-Ernest, an unknown boy, who bravely sacrificed his life for another."

Van Cheele gave way to his aunt in most things, but he flatly refused to subscribe to the Gabriel-Ernest memorial.

# THE HORROR AT CHILTON CASTLE

*JOSEPH PAYNE BRENNAN*

I HAD DECIDED TO SPEND a leisurely summer in Europe, concentrating, if at all, on genealogical research. I went first to Ireland, journeying to Kilkenny, where I unearthed a mine of legend and authentic lore concerning my remote Irish ancestors, the O'Braonains, chiefs of Ui Duach in the ancient kingdom of Ossory. The Brennans (as the name was later spelled) lost their estates in the British confiscation under Thomas Wentworth, Earl of Strafford. The thieving Earl, I am happy to report, was subsequently beheaded in the Tower.

From Kilkenny, I traveled to London and then to Chesterfield in search of maternal ancestors: the Holborns, Wilkersons, Searles, etc. Incomplete and fragmentary records left many great gaps, but my efforts were moderately successful, and at length, I decided to go farther north and visit the vicinity of Chilton Castle, seat of Robert Chilton-Payne, the twelfth Earl of Chilton. My relationship to the Chilton-Paynes was a most distant one, and yet there existed a tenuous thread of past connection, and I thought it would amuse me to glimpse the castle.

Arriving in Wexwold, the tiny village near the castle, late in the afternoon, I engaged a room at the Inn of the Red Goose —the only one there was—unpacked and went down for a simple meal consisting of a small loaf, cheese, and ale.

By the time I finished this stark and yet satisfying repast, darkness had set in, and with it came wind and rain.

I resigned myself to an evening at the inn. There was ale enough and I was in no hurry to go anywhere.

After writing a few letters, I went down and ordered a pint of ale. The taproom was almost deserted; the bartender, a stout gentleman who seemed forever on the point of falling asleep, was pleasant but taciturn, and at length I fell to musing on the strange and frightening legend of Chilton Castle.

There were variations of the legend, and without doubt the original tale had been embroidered down through the centuries, but the essential outline of the story concerned a secret room somewhere in the castle. It was said that this room contained a terrifying spectacle which the Chilton-Paynes were obliged to keep hidden from the world.

Only three persons were ever permitted to enter the room: the residing Earl of Chilton, the Earl's male heir, and one other person designated by the Earl. Ordinarily, this person was the Factor of Chilton Castle. The room was entered only once in a generation; within three days after the male heir came of age, he was conducted to the secret room by the Earl and the Factor. The room was then sealed and never opened again until the heir conducted his own son to the grisly chamber.

According to the legend, the heir was never the same person again after entering the room. Invariably he would become somber and withdrawn; his countenance would acquire a brooding, apprehensive expression which nothing could long dispel. One of the earlier earls of Chilton had gone completely mad and hurled himself from the turrets of the castle.

Speculation about the contents of the secret room had continued for centuries. One version of the tale described the panic-stricken flight of the Gowers, with armed enemies hot on their flagging heels. Although there had been bad blood between the Chilton-Paynes and the Gowers, in their desperation the Gowers begged for refuge at Chilton Castle. The Earl gave them entry, conducted them to the hidden room, and left with a promise that they would be shielded from their pursuers. The Earl kept his promise; the Gowers' enemies were turned away from the Castle, their murderous plans unconsummated. The Earl, however, simply left the Gowers in the locked room to starve to death. The chamber was not opened until thirty years later, when the Earl's son finally broke the seal. A fearful sight met his eyes. The Gowers had starved to death slowly, and at the last, judging by the appearance of the mingled skeletons, had turned to cannibalism.

Another version of the legend indicated that the secret room had been used by medieval earls as a torture chamber. It was said that the ingenious instruments of pain were yet in the room and that these lethal apparatuses still clutched the pitiful remains of their final victims, twisted fearfully in their last agonies.

A third version mentioned one of the female ancestors of the Chilton-Paynes, Lady Susan Glanville, who had reputedly made a pact with the Devil. She had been condemned as a witch, but had somehow managed to escape the stake. The date and even the manner of her death were unknown, but in some vague way the secret room was supposed to be connected with it.

As I speculated on these different versions of the gruesome legend, the storm increased in intensity. Rain drummed steadily against the leaded windows of the inn, and now I could occasionally hear the distant mutter of thunder.

Glancing at the rain-streaked panes, I shrugged and ordered another pint of ale.

I had the fresh tankard halfway to my lips when the taproom door burst open, letting in a blast of wind and rain. The door was shut and a tall figure, muffled to the ears in a dripping greatcoat, moved to the bar. Removing his cap, he ordered brandy.

Having nothing better to do, I observed him closely. He looked about seventy, grizzled and weather-worn, but wiry, with an appearance of toughness and determination. He was frowning, as if absorbed in thinking through some unpleasant problem, yet his cold, blue eyes inspected me keenly for a brief but deliberate interval.

I could not place him in a tidy niche. He might be a local farmer, and yet I did not think that he was. He had a vague aura of authority, and though his clothes were certainly plain, they were, I thought, somewhat better in cut and quality than those of the local countrymen I had observed.

A trivial incident opened a conversation between us. An unusually sharp crack of thunder made him turn toward the window. As he did so, he accidentally brushed his wet cap onto the floor. I retrieved it for him; he thanked me; and then we exchanged commonplace remarks about the weather.

I had an intuitive feeling that although he was normally a reticent individual, he was presently wrestling with some severe problem which made him want to hear a human voice. Realizing there was always the possibility that my intuition might, for once, have failed me, I nevertheless babbled on about my trip, about my genealogical researches in Kilkenny, London, and Chesterfield, and finally about my distant relationship to the Chilton-Paynes and my desire to get a good look at Chilton Castle.

Suddenly, I found that he was gazing at me with an expression which, if not fierce, was disturbingly intense. An awkward silence ensued. I coughed, wondering uneasily what I had said to make those cold, blue eyes stare at me so fixedly.

At length, he became aware of my growing embarrassment. "You must excuse me for staring," he apologized, "but something you said . . ." He hesitated. "Could we perhaps take that table?" He nodded toward a small table which sat half in shadow in the far corner of the room.

I agreed, mystified but curious, and we took our drinks to the secluded table.

He sat frowning for a minute, as if uncertain how to begin. Finally he introduced himself as William Cowath. I gave him my name and still he hesitated. At length he took a swallow of brandy and then looked straight at me. "I am," he stated, "the Factor at Chilton Castle."

I surveyed him with surprise and renewed interest. "What an agreeable coincidence!" I exclaimed. "Then perhaps tomorrow you could arrange for me to have a look at the castle?"

He seemed scarcely to hear me. "Yes, yes, of course," he replied absently.

Puzzled and a bit irritated by his air of detachment, I remained silent.

He took a deep breath and then spoke rapidly, running some of his words together. "Robert Chilton-Payne, the Twelfth Earl of Chilton, was buried in the family vaults one week ago. Frederick, the young heir and now Thirteenth Earl, came of age just three days ago. Tonight it is imperative that he be conducted to the secret chamber!"

I gaped at him in incredulous amazement. For a moment I had an idea that he had somehow heard of my interest in Chilton Castle and was merely "pulling my leg" for amusement, in the belief that I was the greenest of gullible tourists.

But there could be no mistaking his deadly seriousness. There was not the faintest suspicion of humor in his eyes.

I groped for words. "It seems so strange—so unbelievable! Just before you arrived, I had been thinking about the various legends connected with the secret room."

His cold eyes held my own. "It is not legend that confronts us; it is fact."

A thrill of fear and excitement ran through me. "You are going there tonight?"

He nodded. "Tonight. Myself, the young Earl—and one other."

I stared at him.

"Ordinarily," he continued, "the Earl himself would

**171**

accompany us. That is the custom. But he is dead. Shortly before he passed away, he instructed me to select someone to go with the young Earl and myself. That person must be male —and preferably of the blood."

I took a deep drink of ale and said not a word.

He continued. "Besides the young Earl, there is no one at the Castle save his elderly mother, Lady Beatrice Chilton, and an ailing aunt."

"Who could the Earl have had in mind?" I enquired cautiously.

The Factor frowned. "There are some distant male cousins residing in the country. I have an idea he thought at least one of them might appear for the obsequies. But not one of them did."

"That was most unfortunate!" I observed.

"Extremely unfortunate. And I am therefore asking you, as one of the blood, to accompany the young Earl and myself to the secret room tonight!"

I gulped like a bumpkin. Lightning flashed against the windows and I could hear rain swishing along the stones outside. When feathers of ice stopped fluttering in my stomach, I managed a reply.

"But I . . . that is . . . my relationship is so very remote! I am 'of the blood' by courtesy only, you might say. The strain in me is so very diluted."

He shrugged. "You bear the name. And you possess at least a few drops of the Payne blood. Under the present urgent circumstances, no more is necessary. I am sure that the old Earl would agree with me, could he still speak. You will come?"

There was no escaping the intensity, the pressure, of those cold, blue eyes. They seemed to follow my mind about as it groped for further excuses.

Finally, inevitably it seemed, I agreed. A feeling grew in me that the meeting had been preordained, that somehow I had always been destined to visit the secret chamber in Chilton Castle.

We finished our drinks and I went up to my room for

rainwear. When I descended, suitably attired for the storm, the obese bartender was snoring on his stool, in spite of savage crashes of thunder which had now become almost incessant. I envied him as I left the cozy room with William Cowath.

Once outside, my guide informed me that we would have to go on foot to the castle. He had purposely walked down to the inn, he explained, in order that he might have time and solitude to straighten out in his own mind the things which he would have to do.

The sheets of heavy rain, the strong wind, and the roar of thunder made conversation difficult. I walked steps behind the Factor, who took enormous strides and appeared to know every inch of the way in spite of the darkness.

We walked only a short distance down the village street and then struck into a side road, which very soon dwindled to a footpath made slippery and treacherous by the driving rain.

Abruptly, the path began to ascend; the footing became more precarious. It was at once necessary to concentrate all one's attention on one's feet. Fortunately, the flashes of lightning were frequent.

It seemed to me that we had been walking for an hour—actually, I suppose, it was only a few minutes—when the Factor finally stopped.

I found myself standing beside him on a flat, rocky plateau. He pointed up an incline which rose before us. "Chilton Castle," he said.

For a moment I saw nothing in the unrelieved darkness. Then the lightning flashed.

Beyond high battlemented walls, fissured with age, I glimpsed a great, square Norman castle with four rectangular corner towers pierced by narrow window apertures which looked like evil slitted eyes. The huge, weathered pile was half-covered by a mantle of ivy which appeared more black than green.

"It looks incredibly old!" I commented.

William Cowath nodded. "It was begun in 1122 by Henry

173

de Montargis." Without another word, he started up the incline.

As we approached the castle wall, the storm grew worse. The slanting rain and powerful wind now made speech all but impossible. We bent our heads and staggered upward.

When the wall finally loomed in front of us, I was amazed at its height and thickness. It had been constructed, obviously, to withstand the best siege guns and battering rams which its early enemies could bring to bear on it.

As we crossed a massive, timbered drawbridge, I peered down into the black ditch of a moat but I could not be sure whether there was water in it. A low, arched gateway gave access through the wall to an inner, cobblestoned courtyard. This courtyard was entirely empty, save for rivulets of rushing water.

Crossing the cobblestones with swift strides, the Factor led me to another arched gateway in yet another wall. Inside was a second, smaller yard and beyond spread the ivy-clutched base of the ancient keep itself.

Traversing a darkened, stone-flagged passage, we found ourselves facing a ponderous door, age-blackened oak reinforced with pitted bands of iron. The Factor flung open this door, and there before us was the great hall of the castle.

Four long, hand-hewn tables with their accompanying benches stretched almost the entire length of the hall. Metal torch brackets, stained with age, were affixed to sculptured stone columns which supported the roof. Ranged around the walls were suits of armor, heraldic shields, halberds, pikes, and banners—the accumulated trophies and prizes of bloody centuries when each castle was almost a kingdom unto itself. In flickering candlelight, which appeared to be the only illumination, the grim array was eerily impressive.

William Cowath waved a hand, "The holders of Chilton lived by the sword for many centuries."

Walking the length of the great hall, he entered another dim passageway. I followed silently.

As we strode along, he spoke in a subdued voice,

174

"Frederick, the young heir, does not enjoy robust health. The shock of his father's death was severe—and he dreads tonight's ordeal, which he knows must come."

Stopping before a wooden door embellished with carved fleurs-de-lis and metal scrollwork, he gave me a shadowed, enigmatic glance and then knocked.

Someone enquired who was there and he identified himself. Presently a heavy bolt was lifted and the door opened.

If the Chilton-Paynes had been stubborn fighters in their day, the warrior blood appeared to have become considerably diluted in the veins of Frederick, the young heir and now Thirteenth Earl. I saw before me a thin, pale-complexioned young man whose dark, sunken eyes looked haunted and fearful. His dress was both theatrical and anachronistic: a dark-green velvet coat and trousers, a green satin waistband, flounces of white lace at neck and wrists.

He beckoned us in as if with reluctance and closed the door. The walls of the small room were entirely covered with tapestries depicting the hunt or medieval battle scenes. A draft of air from a window or other aperture made them undulate constantly; they seemed to have a disturbing life of their own. In one corner of the room there was an antique canopy bed; in another, a large writing-table with an agate lamp.

After a brief introduction which included an explanation of how I came to be accompanying them, the Factor enquired if his Lordship was ready to visit the chamber.

Although he was wan in any case, Frederick's face now lost every last trace of color. He nodded, however, and preceded us into the passage.

William Cowath led the way; the young Earl followed him, and I brought up the rear.

At the far end of the passage, the Factor opened the door of a cobwebbed supply room. Here he secured candles, chisels, a pick, and a sledgehammer. After packing these into a leather bag which he slung over one shoulder, he picked up a faggot torch which lay on one of the shelves in the room. He lit this, then waited while it flared into a steady flame. Satisfied with this illumination, he closed the room and beckoned for us to continue after him.

Nearby was a descending spiral of stone steps. Lifting his torch, the Factor started down. We trailed after him wordlessly.

There must have been fifty steps in that long, downward spiral. As we descended, the stones became wet and cold; the air, too, grew colder, but the cold was not of the type that refreshes. It was too laden with the smell of mold and dampness.

At the bottom of the steps, we faced a tunnel, pitch-black and silent.

The Factor raised his torch. "Chilton Castle is Norman, but is said to have been reared over a Saxon ruin. It is believed that the passageways in these depths were constructed by the Saxons." He peered, frowning into the tunnel. "Or by some still earlier folk."

He hesitated briefly, and I thought he was listening. Then, glancing around at us, he proceeded down the passage.

I walked after the Earl, shivering. The dead, icy air seemed to pierce to the pith of my bones. The stones underfoot grew slippery with a film of slime. I longed for more light, but there was none save that cast by the flickering, bobbing torch of the Factor.

Partway down the passage he paused, and again I sensed that he was listening. The silence seemed absolute, however, and we went on.

The end of the passage brought us to more descending steps. We went down some fifteen and entered another tunnel which appeared to have been cut out of the solid rock on which the castle had been reared. White-crusted niter clung to the walls. The reek of mold was intense, the icy air was fetid with some other odor which I found peculiarly repellent, though I could not name it.

At last the Factor stopped, lifted his torch, and slid the leather bag from his shoulder.

I saw that we stood before a wall made of some kind of building stone. Though damp and stained with niter, it was obviously of much more recent construction than anything we had previously encountered.

Glancing around at us, William Cowath handed me the torch. "Keep good hold on it, if you please. I have candles, but . . ."

Leaving the sentence unfinished, he drew the pick from his sling bag, and began an assault on the wall. The barrier was solid enough, but after he had worked a hole in it, he took up the sledgehammer and quicker progress was made. Once I offered to take up the hammer while he held the torch, but he only shook his head and went on with his work of demolition.

All this time the young Earl had not spoken a word. As I looked at his tense white face, I felt sorry for him, in spite of my own mounting trepidation.

Abruptly, there was silence as the Factor lowered the sledgehammer. I saw that a good two feet of the lower wall remained.

William Cowath bent to inspect it. "Strong enough," he commented cryptically. "I will leave that to build on. We can step over it."

For a full minute he stood looking silently into the blackness beyond. Finally, shouldering his bag, he took the torch from my hand and stepped over the ragged base of the wall. We followed suit.

As I entered that chamber, the fetid odor which I had noticed in the passage seemed to overwhelm us. It washed around us in a nauseating wave and we all gasped for breath.

The Factor spoke between coughs. "It will subside in a minute or two. Stand near the aperture."

Although the reek remained repellently strong, we could at length breathe more freely.

William Cowath lifted his torch and peered into the black depths of the chamber. Fearfully, I gazed around his shoulder.

There was no sound and at first I could see nothing but niter-encrusted walls and wet stone floor. Presently, however, in a far corner, just beyond the flickering halo of the faggot torch, I saw two tiny, fiery spots of red. I tried to convince myself that they were two red jewels, two rubies, shining in the torchlight.

But I knew at once—I *felt* at once—what they were. They were two red eyes and they were watching us with a fierce, unwavering stare.

The Factor spoke softly. "Wait here."

He crossed toward the corner, stopped halfway, and held out his torch at arm's length. For a moment he was silent. Finally he emitted a long, shuddering sigh.

When he spoke again, his voice had changed. It was only a sepulchral whisper. "Come forward," he told us in that strange, hollow voice.

I followed Frederick until we stood at either side of the Factor.

When I saw what crouched on a stone bench in that far corner, I felt sure that I would faint. My heart literally stopped beating for perceptible seconds. The blood left my extremities; I reeled with dizziness. I might have cried out, but my throat would not open.

The entity which rested on that stone bench was like something that had crawled up out of hell. Piercing, malignant red eyes proclaimed that it had a terrible life, and yet that life sustained itself in a black, shrunken, half-mummified body which resembled a disinterred corpse. A few moldy rags clung to the cadaverlike frame. Wisps of white hair sprouted out of its ghastly gray-white skull. A red smear or blotch of some sort covered the wizened slit which served it as a mouth.

It surveyed us with a malignancy which was beyond anything merely human. It was impossible to stare back into those monstrous red eyes. They were so inexpressibly evil, one felt that one's soul would be consumed in the fires of their malevolence.

Glancing aside, I saw that the Factor was now supporting Frederick. The young heir had sagged against him, staring

fixedly at the fearful apparition with terror-glazed eyes. In spite of my own sense of horror, I pitied him.

The Factor sighed again, and then he spoke once more in that low, sepulchral voice.

"You see before you," he told us, "Lady Susan Glanville. She was carried into this chamber and then fettered to the wall in 1473."

A thrill of horror coursed through me; I felt that we were in the presence of malign forces from the Pit itself.

To me the hideous thing had appeared sexless, but at the sound of its name, the ghastly mockery of a grin contorted the puckered, red-smeared mouth.

I noticed now for the first time that the monster actually was secured to the wall. The great double shackles were so blackened with age, I had not noticed them before.

The Factor went on, as if he spoke by rote. "Lady Glanville was a maternal ancestor of the Chilton-Paynes. She had commerce with the Devil. She was condemned as a witch but escaped the stake. Finally her own people forcibly overcame her. She was brought in here, fettered, and left to die."

He was silent a moment and then continued. "It was too late. She had already made a pact with the Powers of Darkness. It was an unspeakably evil thing and it has condemned her issue to a life of torment and nightmare, a lifetime of terror and dread."

He swung his torch toward the blackened, red-eyed thing. "She was a beauty once. She hated death. She feared death. And so she finally bartered her own immortal soul—and the bodies of her issue—for eternal, earthly life."

I heard his voice as in a nightmare; it seemed to be coming from an infinite distance.

He went on. "The consequences of breaking the pact are too terrible to describe. No descendant of hers has ever dared to do so, once the forfeit is known. And so she had bided here for these nearly five hundred years."

I had thought he was finished, but he resumed. Glancing upward, he lifted his torch toward the roof of that accursed

180

chamber. "This room," he said, "lies directly underneath the family vaults. Upon the death of the Earl, the body is ostensibly left in the vaults. When the mourners have gone, however, the false bottom of the vault is thrust aside and the body of the Earl is lowered into this room."

Looking up, I saw the square rectangle of a trapdoor above.

The Factor's voice now became barely audible. "Once every generation Lady Glanville feeds—on the corpse of the deceased Earl. It is a provision of that unspeakable pact which cannot be broken."

I knew now—with a sense of horror utterly beyond description—whence came that red smear on the repulsive mouth of the creature before us.

As if to confirm his words, the Factor lowered his torch until its flame illuminated the floor at the foot of the stone bench where the vampiric monster was fettered.

Strewn around the floor were the scattered bones and skull of an adult male, red with fresh blood. And at some distance were other human bones, brown, and crumbling with age.

At this point, Frederick began to scream. His shrill, hysterical cries filled the chamber. Although the Factor shook him roughly, his terrible shrieks continued, terror-filled, nerve-shaking.

For moments, the corpselike thing on the bench watched him with its frightful red eyes. It uttered sound finally, a kind of animal squeal which might have been intended as laughter.

Abruptly then, and without any warning, it slid from the bench and lunged toward the young Earl. The blackened shackles which fettered it to the wall permitted it to advance only a yard or two. It was pulled back sharply; yet it lunged again and again, squealing with a kind of hellish glee which stirred the hair on my head.

William Cowath thrust his torch toward the monster, but it continued to lunge at the end of its fetters. The nightmare room resounded with the Earl's screams and the creature's horrible squeals of bestial laughter. I felt that my own mind would give way unless I escaped from that anteroom of hell.

For the first time during an ordeal which would have sent any lesser man fleeing for his life and sanity, the iron control of the Factor appeared to be shaken. He looked beyond the wild lunging thing toward the wall where the fetters were fastened.

I sensed what was in his mind. Would those fastenings hold, after all these centuries of rust and dampness?

On a sudden resolve, he reached into an inner pocket and drew out something which glittered in the torchlight. It was a silver crucifix. Striding forward, he thrust it almost into the twisted face of the leaping monstrosity which had once been the ravishing Lady Susan Glanville.

The creature reeled back with an agonized scream which drowned out the cries of the Earl. It cowered on the bench, abruptly silent and motionless, only the pulsating of its wizened mouth and the fires of hatred in its red eyes giving evidence that it still lived.

William Cowath addressed it grimly. "Creature of hell! If ye leave that bench ere we quit this room and seal it once again, I swear that I shall hold this cross against ye!"

The thing's red eyes watched the Factor with an expression of abysmal hatred which no combination of mere letters could convey. They actually appeared to glow with fire. And yet I read in them something else—fear.

I suddenly became aware that silence had descended on that room of the damned. It lasted only a few moments. The Earl had finally stopped screaming, but now came something worse. He began to laugh.

It was only a low chuckle, but it was somehow worse than all his screams. It went on and on, softly, mindlessly.

The Factor turned, beckoning me toward the partially demolished wall. Crossing the room, I climbed out. Behind me, the Factor led the young Earl, who shuffled like an old man, chuckling to himself.

There was then what seemed an interminable interval, during which the Factor carried back a sack of mortar and a keg of water which he had previously left somewhere in the tunnel. Working by torchlight, he prepared the cement and proceeded to seal up the chamber, using the same stones which he had displaced.

While the Factor labored, the young Earl sat motionless in the tunnel, chuckling softly.

There was silence from within. Once, only, I heard the thing's fetters clank against the stone.

At last, the Factor finished and led us back through those niter-stained passageways and up the icy stairs. The Earl could scarcely ascend; with difficulty, the Factor supported him from step to step.

Back in his tapestry-paneled chamber, Frederick sat on his canopy bed and stared at the floor, laughing quietly. With horror, I noticed that the black hair had actually turned gray. After persuading him to drink a glass of liquid which I had no doubt contained a heavy dose of sedative, the Factor managed to get him stretched out on the bed.

William Cowath then led me to a nearby bedchamber. My impulse was to rush from that hellish pile without delay, but the storm still raged and I was by no means sure I could find my way back to the village without a guide.

The Factor shook his head sadly. "I fear his Lordship is doomed to an early death. He was never strong and tonight's events may have deranged his mind . . . may have weakened him beyond hope of recovery."

I expressed my sympathy and horror. The Factor's cold, blue eyes held my own. "It may be," he said, "that in the event of the young Earl's death, you yourself might be considered . . . ." He hesitated. "Might be considered," he finally concluded, "as one somewhat in the line of succession."

I wanted to hear no more. I gave him a curt goodnight, bolted the door after him and tried—quite unsuccessfully—to salvage a few minutes' sleep.

But sleep would not come. I had feverish visions of that red-eyed thing in the sealed chamber escaping its fetters, breaking through the wall and crawling up those icy, slime-covered stairs . . . .

Even before dawn, I softly unbolted my door and, like a marauding thief, crept shivering through the cold passageways and the great deserted hall of the castle. Crossing the cobbled courtyards and the black moat, I scrambled down the incline toward the village.

Long before noon I was well on my way to London. Luck was with me; the next day, I was on a boat bound for the Atlantic run.

I shall never return to England. I intend always to keep Chilton Castle and its permanent occupant at least an ocean away.

# COUNT DRACULA

*WOODY ALLEN*

S OMEWHERE IN TRANSYLVANIA, Dracula the monster lies
sleeping in his coffin, waiting for night to fall. As
exposure to the sun's rays would surely cause him to
perish, he stays protected in the satin-lined chamber bearing
his family name in silver. Then the moment of darkness
comes, and through some miraculous instinct, the fiend
emerges from the safety of his hiding-place and, assuming
the hideous form of the bat or the wolf, he prowls the
countryside, drinking the blood of his victims. Finally, before
the first rays of his arch-enemy, the sun, announce a new day,
he hurries back to the safety of his hidden coffin and sleeps,
as the cycle begins anew.

Now he starts to stir. The fluttering of his eyelids is a
response to some age-old, unexplainable instinct that the sun
is nearly down and his time is near. Tonight, he is particularly
hungry and as he lies there, fully awake now, in red-lined
Inverness cape and tails, waiting to feel with uncanny
perception the precise moment of darkness before opening
the lid and emerging, he decides who this evening's victims
will be. The baker and his wife, he thinks to himself.
Succulent, available, and unsuspecting. The thought of the

185

unwary couple whose trust he has carefully cultivated excites his blood lust to fever pitch, and he can barely hold back these last seconds before climbing out of the coffin to seek his prey.

Suddenly, he knows the sun is down. Like an angel of hell, he rises swiftly and, changing into a bat, flies pell-mell to the cottage of his tantalizing victims.

"Why, Count Dracula, what a nice surprise," the baker's wife says, opening the door to admit him. (He has once again assumed human form as he enters their home, charmingly concealing his rapacious goal.)

"What brings you here so early?" the baker asks.

"Our dinner date," the Count answers. "I hope I haven't made an error. You did invite me for tonight, didn't you?"

"Yes, tonight, but that's not for seven hours."

"Pardon me?" Dracula queries, looking around the room puzzled.

"Or did you come by to watch the eclipse with us?"

"Eclipse?"

"Yes. Today's the total eclipse."

"What?"

"A few moments of darkness from noon until two minutes after. Look out the window."

"Uh-oh—I'm in big trouble."

"Eh?"

"And now if you'll excuse me . . . ."

"What, Count Dracula?"

"Must be going—aha—oh, god . . . ." Frantically, he fumbles for the door knob.

"Going? You just came."

"Yes—but—I think I blew it very badly . . . ."

"Count Dracula, you're pale."

"Am I? I need a little fresh air. It was nice seeing you . . ."

"Come. Sit down. We'll have a drink."

"Drink? No, I must run. Er—you're stepping on my cape."

"Sure. Relax. Some wine."

"Wine? Oh no, gave it up—liver and all that, you know.

And now I really must buzz off. I just remembered, I left the lights on at my castle—bills'll be enormous . . . ."

"Please," the baker says, his arm around the Count in firm friendship. "You're not intruding. Don't be so polite. So you're early."

"Really, I'd like to stay, but there's a meeting of old Roumanian Counts across town and I'm responsible for the cold cuts."

"Rush, rush, rush. It's a wonder you don't get a heart attack."

"Yes, right—and now—"

"I'm making Chicken Pilaf tonight," the baker's wife chimes in. "I hope you like it."

"Wonderful, wonderful," the Count says with a smile, as he pushes her aside into some laundry. Then, opening a closet door by mistake, he walks in. "Christ, where's the goddamn front door?"

"Ach," laughs the baker's wife, "such a funny man, the Count."

"I knew you'd like that," Dracula says, forcing a chuckle, "now get out of my way." At last he opens the front door, but time has run out on him.

"Oh, look, mama," says the baker, "the eclipse must be over. The sun is coming out again."

"Right," says Dracula, slamming the front door. "I've decided to stay. Pull down the window shades quickly— quickly! Let's move it!"

"What window shades?" asks the baker.

"There are none, right? Figures. You got a basement in this joint?"

"No," says the wife affably, "I'm always telling Jarslov to build one but he never listens. That's some Jarslov, my husand."

"I'm all choked up. Where's the closet?"

"You did that one already, Count Dracula. Unt mama and I laughed at it."

"Ach—such a funny man, the Count."

"Look, I'll be in the closet. Knock at seven-thirty." And with that, the Count steps inside the closet and slams the door.

"Hee-hee—he is so funny, Jarslov."

"Oh, Count. Come out of the closet. Stop being a big silly." From inside the closet comes the muffled voice of Dracula.

"Can't—please—take my word for it. Just let me stay here. I'm fine. Really."

"Count Dracula, stop the fooling. We're already helpless with laughter."

"Can I tell you, I love this closet."

"Yes, but . . ."

"I know, I know . . . it seems strange, and yet here I am, having a ball. I was just saying to Mrs. Hess the other day, give me a good closet and I can stand in it for hours. Sweet woman, Mrs. Hess. Fat but sweet . . . Now, why don't you run along and check back with me at sunset. Oh, Ramona, la da da de da da de, Ramona . . . ."

Now the Mayor and his wife, Katia, arrive. They are passing by and have decided to pay a call on their good friends, the baker and his wife.

"Hello, Jarslov. I hope Katia and I are not intruding?"

"Of course not, Mr. Mayor. Come out, Count Dracula! We have company!"

"Is the Count here?" asks the Mayor, surprised.

"Yes, and you'll never guess where," says the baker's wife.

"It's so rare to see him around this early. In fact I can't ever remember seeing him around in the daytime."

"Well, he's here. Come out, Count Dracula!"

"Where is he?" Katia asks, not knowing whether to laugh or not.

"Come on out now! Let's go!" The baker's wife is getting impatient.

"He's in the closet," says the baker, apologetically.

"Really?" asks the Mayor.

"Let's go," says the baker with mock good humor as he knocks on the closet door. "Enough is enough. The Mayor's here."

"Come on out, Dracula," His Honor shouts, "let's have a drink."

"No, go ahead. I've got some business in here."

"In the closet?"

"Yes, don't let me spoil your day. I can hear what you're saying. I'll join in if I have anything to add."

Everyone looks at one another and shrugs. Wine is poured and they all drink.

"Some eclipse today," the Mayor says, sipping from his glass.

"Yes," the baker agrees. "Incredible."

"Yeah. Thrilling," says a voice from the closet.

"What, Dracula?"

"Nothing, nothing. Let it go."

And so the time passes, until the Mayor can stand it no longer and, forcing open the door to the closet, he shouts, "Come on, Dracula. I always thought you were a mature man. Stop this craziness."

The daylight streams in, causing the evil monster to shriek and slowly dissolve to a skeleton and then to dust before the eyes of the four people present. Leaning down to the pile of white ash on the closet floor, the baker's wife shouts, "Does this mean dinner's off tonight?"

# THE WEREWOLF

*ANGELA CARTER*

IT IS A NORTHERN COUNTRY; they have cold weather, they have cold hearts.

Cold; tempest; wild beasts in the forest. It is a hard life. Their houses are built of logs, dark and smoky within. There will be a crude icon of the Virgin behind a guttering candle, the leg of a pig hung up to cure, and a string of drying mushrooms. A bed, a stool, a table. Harsh, brief, poor lives.

To these upland woodsmen, the Devil is as real as you or I. More so; they have not seen us nor even know that we exist, but the Devil they glimpse often in the graveyards, those bleak and touching townships of the dead where the graves are marked with portraits of the deceased in the naïf style and there are no flowers to put in front of them, no flowers grow there, so they put out small, votive offerings, little loaves, sometimes a cake that the bears come lumbering from the margins of the forest to snatch away. At midnight, especially on Walpurgisnacht, the Devil holds picnics in the graveyards and invites the witches; then they dig up fresh corpses, and eat them. Anyone will tell you that.

Wreaths of garlic on the doors keep out the vampires. A blue-eyed child born feet-first on the night of St. John's Eve will have second sight. When they discover a witch—some old woman whose cheeses ripen when her neighbors' do not, another old woman whose black cat, oh, sinister! *follows her around all the time*, they strip the crone, search for her marks, for the supernumerary nipple her familiar sucks. They soon find it. Then they stone her to death.

Winter and cold weather.

"Go and visit grandmother, who has been sick. Take her the oatcakes I've baked for her on the hearthstone, and a little pot of butter."

The good child does as her mother bids—five miles' trudge through the forest; do not leave the path because of the bears, the wild boar, the starving wolves. "Here, take your father's hunting knife; you know how to use it."

The child had a scabby coat of sheepskin to keep out the cold, she knew the forest too well to fear it, but she must always be on her guard. When she heard that freezing howl of a wolf, she dropped her gifts, seized her knife, and turned on the beast.

It was a huge one, with red eyes and running, grizzled chops; any but a mountaineer's child would have died of fright at the sight of it. It went for her throat, as wolves do, but she made a great swipe at it with her father's knife and slashed off its right forepaw.

The wolf let out a gulp, almost a sob, when it saw what had happened to it; wolves are less brave than they seem. It went lolloping off disconsolately between the trees as well as it could on three legs, leaving a trail of blood behind it. The child wiped the blade of her knife clean on her apron, wrapped up the wolf's paw in the cloth in which her mother had packed the oatcakes, and went on toward her grandmother's house. Soon it came on to snow so thickly that the path and any footsteps, track, or spoor that might have been upon it were obscured.

She found her grandmother was so sick that she had taken to her bed and fallen into a fretful sleep, moaning and shaking so that the child guessed she had a fever. She felt the forehead,

it burned. She shook out the cloth from her basket, to use it to make the old woman a cold compress, and the wolf's paw fell to the floor.

But it was no longer a wolf's paw. It was a hand, chopped off at the wrist, a hand toughened with work and freckled with old age. There was a wedding ring on the third finger and a wart on the index finger. By the wart, she knew it for her grandmother's hand.

She pulled back the sheet, but the old woman woke up at that and began to struggle, squawking and shrieking like a thing possessed. But the child was strong, and armed with her father's hunting knife, she managed to hold her grandmother down long enough to see the cause of her fever. There was a bloody stump where her right hand should have been, festering already.

The child crossed herself and cried out so loud the neighbors heard her and came rushing in. They knew the wart on the hand at once for a witch's nipple; they drove the old woman, in her shift as she was, out into the snow with sticks, beating her old carcass as far as the edge of the forest, and pelted her with stones until she fell down dead.

Now the child lived in her grandmother's house; she prospered.

# THE DRIFTING SNOW

*AUGUST DERLETH*

AUNT MARY'S advancing footsteps halted suddenly, short of the table, and Clodetta turned to see what was keeping her. She was standing very rigidly, her eyes fixed upon the French windows just opposite the door through which she had entered, her cane held stiffly before her.

Clodetta shot a quick glance across the table toward her husband, whose attention had also been drawn to his aunt; his face vouchsafed her nothing. She turned again to find that the old lady had transferred her gaze to her, regarding her stonily and in silence. Clodetta felt uncomfortable.

"Who withdrew the curtains from the west windows?"

Clodetta flushed, remembering. "I did, Aunt. I'm sorry. I forgot about your not wanting them drawn away."

The old lady made an odd, grunting sound, shifting her gaze once again to the French windows. She made a barely perceptible movement, and Lisa ran forward from the shadow of the hall, where she had been regarding the two at table with stern disapproval. The servant went directly to the west windows and drew the curtains.

Aunt Mary came slowly to the table and took her place at

its head. She put her cane against the side of her chair, pulled at the chain around her neck so that her lorgnette lay in her lap, and looked from Clodetta to her nephew, Ernest.

Then she fixed her gaze on the empty chair at the foot of the table, and spoke without seeming to see the two beside her. "I told both of you that none of the curtains over the west windows was to be withdrawn after sundown, and you must have noticed that none of those windows has been for one instant uncovered at night. I took especial care to put you in rooms facing east, and the sitting room is also in the east."

"I'm sure Clodetta didn't mean to go against your wishes, Aunt Mary," said Ernest abruptly.

"No, of course not, Aunt."

The old lady raised her eyebrows, and went on impassively. "I didn't think it wise to explain why I made such a request. I'm not going to explain. But I do want to say that there is a very definite danger in drawing away the curtains. Ernest has heard that before, but you, Clodetta, have not."

Clodetta shot a startled glance at her husband. The old lady caught it, and said, "It's all very well to believe that my mind's wandering or that I'm getting eccentric, but I shouldn't advise you to be satisfied with that."

A young man came suddenly into the room and made for the seat at the foot of the table, into which he flung himself with an almost inaudible greeting to the other three.

"Late again, Henry," said the old lady.

Henry mumbled something and began hurriedly to eat. The old lady sighed, and began presently to eat also, whereupon Clodetta and Ernest did likewise. The old servant, who had continued to linger behind Aunt Mary's chair, now withdrew, not without a scornful glance at Henry.

Clodetta looked up after a while and ventured to speak. "You aren't as isolated as I thought you might be up here, Aunt Mary."

"We aren't, my dear, what with telephones and cars and all. But only twenty years ago it was quite a different thing, I can tell you." She smiled reminiscently and looked at Ernest.

196

"Your grandfather was living then, and many's the time he was snowbound with no way to let anybody know."

"Down in Chicago, when they speak of 'up north' or the 'Wisconsin woods' it seems very far away," said Clodetta.

"Well, it *is* far away," put in Henry, abruptly. "And, Aunt, I hope you've made some provision in case we're locked in here for a day or two. It looks like snow outside, and the radio says a blizzard's coming."

The old lady grunted and looked at him. "Ha, Henry—you're overly concerned, it seems to me. I'm afraid you've been regretting this trip ever since you set foot in my house. If you're worrying about a snowstorm, I can have Sam drive you down to Wausau, and you can be in Chicago tomorrow."

"Of course not."

Silence fell, and presently the old lady called gently, "Lisa," and the servant came into the room to help her from her chair, though, as Clodetta had previously said to her husband, "She didn't need help."

From the doorway, Aunt Mary bade them all goodnight, looking impressively formidable with her cane in one hand and her unopened lorgnette in the other, and vanished into the dusk of the hall, from which her receding footsteps sounded together with those of the servant, who was seldom seen away from her. These two were alone in the house most of the time, and only very brief periods when the old lady had up her nephew Ernest, "dear John's boy," or Henry, of whose father the old lady never spoke, helped to relieve the pleasant somnolence of their quiet lives. Sam, who usually slept in the garage, did not count.

Clodetta looked nervously at her husband, but it was Henry who said what was uppermost in their thoughts.

"I think she's losing her mind," he declared matter-of-factly. Cutting off Clodetta's protest on her lips, he got up and went into the sitting room, from which came presently the strains of music from the radio.

Clodetta fingered her spoon idly and finally said, "I do think she is a little queer Ernest."

197

Ernest smiled tolerantly. "No, I don't think so. I've an idea why she keeps the west windows covered. My grandfather died out there—he was overcome by the cold one night, and froze on the slope of the hill. I don't rightly know how it happened—I was away at the time. I suppose she doesn't like to be reminded of it."

"But where's the danger she spoke of, then?"

He shrugged. "Perhaps it lies in her—she might be affected and affect us in turn." He paused for an instant, and finally added, "I suppose she *does* seem a little strange to you —but she was like that as long as I can remember; next time you come, you'll be used to it."

Clodetta looked at her husband for a moment before replying. At last she said, "I don't think I like the house, Ernest."

"Oh, nonsense, darling." He started to get up, but Clodetta stopped him.

"Listen, Ernest. I remembered perfectly well Aunt Mary's not wanting those curtains drawn away—but I just felt I had to do it. I didn't want to, but—*something made me do it*." Her voice was unsteady.

"Why, Clodetta," he said, faintly alarmed. "Why didn't you tell me before?"

She shrugged. "Aunt Mary might have thought I'd gone wool-gathering."

"Well, it's nothing serious, but you've let it bother you a little and that isn't good for you. Forget it; think of something else. Come and listen to the radio."

They rose and moved toward the sitting room together. At the door Henry met them. He stepped aside a little, saying, "I might have known we'd be marooned up here," and adding, as Clodetta began to protest, "We're going to be alright. There's a wind coming up and it's beginning to snow, and I know what that means." He passed them and went into the deserted dining room, where he stood a moment looking at the too-long table. Then he turned aside and went over to the French windows, from which he drew away the curtains and stood there peering out into the darkness. Ernest saw him standing at the window, and protested from the sitting room.

"Aunt Mary doesn't like those windows uncovered, Henry."

Henry half turned and replied, "Well, *she* may think it's dangerous, but I can risk it."

Clodetta, who had been staring beyond Henry into the night through the French windows, said suddenly, "Why, there's someone out there!"

Henry looked quickly through the glass and replied, "No, that's the snow; it's coming down heavily, and the wind's drifting it this way and that." He dropped the curtains and came away from the windows.

Clodetta said uncertainly, "Why, I could have sworn I saw someone out there, walking past the window."

"I suppose it does look that way from here," offered Henry, who had come back into the sitting room. "But personally, I think you've let Aunt Mary's eccentricities impress you too much."

Ernest made an impatient gesture at this, and Clodetta did not answer. Henry sat down before the radio and began to move the dial slowly. Ernest had found himself a book, and was becoming interested, but Clodetta continued to sit with her eyes fixed upon the still slowly-moving curtains cutting off the French windows. Presently she got up and left the room, going down the long hall into the east wing, where she tapped gently upon Aunt Mary's door.

"Come in," called the old lady.

Clodetta opened the door and stepped into the room where Aunt Mary sat in her dressing robe, her dignity, in the shape of her lorgnette and cane, resting respectively on her bureau and in the corner. She looked surprisingly benign, as Clodetta at once confessed.

"Ha, thought I was an ogre in disguise, did you?" said the old lady, smiling in spite of herself. "I'm really not, you see, but I am a sort of bogey about the west windows, as you have seen."

"I wanted to tell you something about those windows, Aunt Mary," said Clodetta. She stopped suddenly. The expression on the old lady's face had given way to a curiously dismaying one. It was not anger, not distaste—it was a lurking suspense. Why, the old lady was afraid!

"What?" she asked Clodetta shortly.

"I was looking out—just for a moment or so—and I thought I saw someone out there."

"Of course, you didn't, Clodetta. Your imagination, perhaps, or the drifting snow."

"My imagination? Maybe. But there was no wind to drift the snow, though one has come up since."

"I've often been fooled that way, my dear. Sometimes I've gone out in the morning to look for footprints—there weren't any, ever. We're pretty far away from civilization in a snowstorm, despite our telephones and radios. Our nearest neighbor is at the foot of the long, sloping rise—over three miles away—and all wooded land between. There's no highway nearer than that."

"It was so clear, I could have sworn to it."

"Do you want to go out in the morning and look?" asked the old lady shortly.

"Of course not."

"Then you didn't see anything."

It was half-question, half-demand. Clodetta said, "Oh, Aunt Mary, you're making an issue of it now."

"Did you or didn't you in your own mind see anything, Clodetta?"

"I guess I didn't, Aunt Mary."

"Very well. And now do you think we might talk about something more pleasant?"

"Why, I'm sure—I'm sorry, Aunt. I didn't know that Ernest's grandfather had died out there."

"Ha, he's told you that, has he? Well?"

"Yes, he said that was why you didn't like the slope after sunset—that you didn't like to be reminded of his death."

The old lady looked at Clodetta impassively.

"Perhaps he'll never know how nearly right he was."

"What do you mean, Aunt Mary?"

"Nothing for you to know, my dear." She smiled again, her sternness dropping from her. "And now I think you'd better go, Clodetta; I'm tired."

Clodetta rose obediently and made for the door, where the old lady stopped her. "How's the weather?"

"It's snowing—hard, Henry says—and blowing."

The old lady's face showed her distaste at the news. "I don't like to hear that, not at all. Suppose someone should look down that slope tonight?" She was speaking to herself, having forgotten Clodetta at the door. Seeing her again abruptly, she said, "But you don't know, Clodetta. Goodnight."

Clodetta stood with her back against the closed door, wondering what the old lady could have meant. *But you don't know, Clodetta.* That was curious. For a moment or two the old lady had completely forgotten her.

She moved away from the door, and came upon Ernest just turning into the east wing.

"Oh, there you are," he said. "I wondered where you had gone."

"I was talking a bit with Aunt Mary."

"Henry's been at the west windows again—and now *he* thinks there's someone out there."

Clodetta stopped short. "Does he really think so?"

Ernest nodded gravely. "But the snow's drifting frightfully, and I can imagine how that suggestion of yours worked on his mind."

Clodetta turned and went back along the hall. "I'm going to tell Aunt Mary."

He started to protest, but to no avail, for she was already tapping on the old lady's door, and indeed opening the door and entering the room before he could frame an adequate protest.

"Aunt Mary," she said, "I didn't want to disturb you again, but Henry's been at the French windows in the dining room,

202

and he says he's seen someone out there."

The effect on the old lady was magical. "He's seen them!" she exclaimed. Then she was on her feet, coming rapidly over to Clodetta. "How long ago?" she demanded, seizing her almost roughly by the arms. "Tell me, quickly. How long ago did he see them?"

Clodetta's amazement kept her silent for a moment, but at last she spoke, feeling the old lady's keen eyes staring at her. "It was some time ago, Aunt Mary, after supper."

The old lady's hands relaxed, and with it her tension. "Oh," she said, and turned and went back slowly to her chair, taking her cane from the corner where she had put it for the night.

"Then there *is* someone out there?" challenged Clodetta, when the old lady had reached her chair.

For a long time, it seemed to Clodetta, there was no answer. Then presently, the old lady began to nod gently, and a barely audible "yes" escaped her lips.

"Then we had better take them in, Aunt Mary."

The old lady looked at Clodetta earnestly for a moment; then she replied, her voice firm and low, her eyes fixed upon the wall beyond. "We can't take them in, Clodetta—because they're not alive."

At once Henry's words came flashing into Clodetta's memory—"She's losing her mind,"—and her involuntary start betrayed her thought.

"I'm afraid I'm not mad, my dear—I hoped at first I might be, but I wasn't. I'm not, now. There was only one of them out there at first—the girl; Father is the other. Quite long ago, when I was young, my father did something which he regretted all his days. He had a too strong temper, and it maddened him. One night, he found out that one of my brothers—Henry's father—had been very familiar with one of the servants, a very pretty girl, older than I was. He thought she was to blame, though she wasn't, and he didn't find it out until too late. He drove her from the house, then and there. Winter had not yet set in, but it was quite cold, and she had some five miles to go to her home. We begged Father not to

203

send her away—though we didn't know what was wrong then—but he paid no attention to us. The girl had to go.

"Not long after she had gone, a biting wind came up, and close upon it a fierce storm. Father had already repented his hasty action, and sent some of the men to look for the girl. They didn't find her, but in the morning she was found frozen to death on the long slope of the hill to the west."

The old lady sighed, paused a moment, and went on. "Years later—she came back. She came in a snowstorm, as she went; but she had become a vampire. We all saw her. We were at supper table, and Father saw her first. The boys had already gone upstairs, and Father and the two of us girls, my sister and I, did not recognize her. She was just a dim shape floundering around in the drifting snow beyond the French windows. Father ran out to her, calling to us to send the boys after him. We never saw him alive again. In the morning we found him in the same spot where years before the girl had been found. He, too, had died of exposure.

"Then, a few years after—she returned with the snow, and she brought him along; he, too, had become a vampire. They stayed until the last snow, always trying to lure someone out there. After that, I knew, and had the windows covered during the winter nights, from sunset to dawn, because they never went beyond the west slope.

"Now you know, Clodetta."

Whatever Clodetta was going to say was cut short by running footsteps in the hall, a hasty rap, and Ernest's head appearing suddenly in the open doorway.

"Come on, you two," he said, almost gaily, "there *are* people out on the west slope—a girl and an old man—and Henry's gone out to fetch them in!"

Then, triumphant, he was off. Clodetta came to her feet, but the old lady was before her, passing her and almost running down the hall, calling loudly for Lisa, who presently appeared in nightcap and gown from her room.

"Call Sam, Lisa," said the old lady, "and send him to me in the dining room."

She ran on into the dining room, Clodetta close on her heels. The French windows were open, and Ernest stood on the snow-covered terrace beyond, calling his cousin. The old lady went directly over to him, even striding into the snow to his side, though the wind drove the snow against her with great force. The wooded western slope was lost in a snow-fog; the nearest trees were barely discernible.

"Where could they have gone?" Ernest said, turning to the old lady, whom he had thought to be Clodetta. Then, seeing that it was the old lady, he said, "Why, Aunt Mary—and so little on, too! You'll catch your death of cold."

"Never mind, Ernest," said the old lady. "I'm all right. I've had Sam get up to help you look for Henry—but I'm afraid you won't find him."

"He can't be far; he just now went out."

"He went before you saw where; he's far enough gone."

Sam came running into the blowing snow from the dining room, muffled in a greatcoat. He was considerably older than Ernest, almost the old lady's age. He shot a questioning glance at her and asked, "Have they come again?"

Aunt Mary nodded. "You'll have to look for Henry. Ernest will help you. And remember, don't separate. And don't go far from the house."

Clodetta came with Ernest's overcoat, and together the two women stood there, watching them until they were swallowed up in the wall of driven snow. Then they turned slowly, and went back into the house.

The old lady sank into a chair facing the windows. She was pale and drawn, and looked, as Clodetta said afterward, "as if she'd fallen together." For a long time she said nothing. Then, with a gentle little sigh, she turned to Clodetta and spoke.

"Now there'll be three of them out there."

Then, so suddenly that no one knew how it happened, Ernest and Sam appeared beyond the windows, and between them they dragged Henry. The old lady flew to open the windows, and the three of them, cloaked in snow, came into the room.

205

"We found him—but the cold's hit him pretty hard, I'm afraid," said Ernest.

The old lady sent Lisa for cold water, and Ernest ran to get himself other clothes. Clodetta went with him, and in their rooms told him what the old lady had related to her.

Ernest laughed. "I think you believed that, didn't you, Clodetta? Sam and Lisa do, I know, because Sam told me the story long ago. I think the shock of Grandfather's death was too much for all three of them."

"But the story of the girl, and then—"

"That part's true, I'm afraid. A nasty story, but it did happen."

"But those people Henry and I saw!" protested Clodetta weakly.

Ernest stood without movement. "That's so," he said, "I saw them, too. Then they're out there yet, and we'll have to find them!" He took up his overcoat again, and went from the room, Clodetta protesting in a shrill unnatural voice. The old lady met him at the door of the dining room, having overheard Clodetta pleading with him.

"No, Ernest—you can't go out there again," she said. "There's no one there."

He pushed gently into the room and called to Sam. "Coming, Sam? There's still two of them out there—we almost forgot them."

Sam looked at him strangely. "What do you mean?" he demanded roughly. He looked challengingly at the old lady, who shook her head.

"The girl and the old man, Sam. We've got to get them, too."

"Oh, *them*," said Sam. "They're dead!"

"Then I'll go out alone," said Ernest.

Henry came to his feet suddenly, looking dazed. He walked forward a few steps, his eyes travelling from one to the other of them, yet apparently not seeing them. He began to speak abruptly, in an unnatural, childlike voice.

"*The snow,*" he murmured, "*the snow—the beautiful hands, so little, so lovely—her beautiful hands—and the snow, the beautiful,*"

206

*lovely snow, drifting and falling around her . . . ."*

He turned slowly and looked toward the French windows, the others following his gaze. Beyond was a wall of white, where the snow was drifting against the house. For a moment Henry stood quietly watching, then suddenly a white figure came forward from the snow—a young girl, cloaked in long snow-whips, her glistening eyes strangely fascinating.

The old lady flung herself forward, her arms outstretched to cling to Henry, but she was too late. Henry had run toward the windows, had opened them, and even as Clodetta cried out, had vanished into the wall of snow beyond.

Then Ernest ran forward, but the old lady threw her arms around him and held him tightly, murmuring, "You shall not go! Henry is gone beyond our help!"

Clodetta came to help her, and Sam stood menacingly at the French windows, now closed against the wind and the sinister snow. So they held him, and would not let him go.

"And tomorrow," said the old lady in a harsh whisper, "we must go to their graves and stake them down. We should have gone before."

In the morning they found Henry's body crouched against the bole of an ancient oak, where the two others had been found years before. There were almost obliterated marks of where something had dragged him, a long, uneven swath in the snow, and yet no footprints, only strange, hollowed places along the way, as if the wind had whirled the snow away, and only the wind.

But on his skin were signs of the snow vampire—the delicate small prints of a young girl's hands.

# HOWL

*ALAN DURANT*

DAD MOVED OUT to the Park after Mom died. I was only a young kid at the time and didn't know much about anything. I don't recall really missing Mom, but, like I say, I was very small—just a baby. The truth is, I don't think I ever knew Mom well enough to miss her.

Dad and I had always been very close—which was lucky, I guess, seeing as we lived such an isolated existence. We lived right in the heart of Wilderness Park, twenty acres of moorland. Dad was the Warden, and there were no other inhabitants for about ten miles all around. At least there weren't, till the Travellers came. They arrived one night in their trucks and caravans and made themselves a camp by Monks' Burn, just a mile away from us. Dad was furious. The next morning when he saw them, there was an almighty row. He and their leader, Vincent, practically came to blows. I mean, Dad was right, I guess. They shouldn't have been there. It's against the law and it was his job to say so. But it went deeper than that. Dad had got a real mania for privacy. I mean he wouldn't even let people come near our house. Once or twice I'd asked him if I could have a schoolmate to stay the night, but the answer had always been no. He said he was on call the whole time—day and night—and he couldn't take responsibility for looking after guests too. But I knew there was more to it than that.

"My friends are fourteen years old, Dad," I said to him the last time. "They don't need looking after."

But Dad shook his head, and his blue eyes were so light and piercing I couldn't bear to look at them. "They need looking after all right, Lucas," he said with a bitterness I didn't understand. But then Dad was a mystery. Away from the Park, when we went out shopping and stuff, he was as amiable and charming as anyone could be. You'd think he was the world's most sociable guy; the sort of person you'd expect to see drinking in the pub or down at the match with his pals. But as soon as we were back in the Park, he became this other being: intense, brooding, private. A real lone wolf. I'd seen him sometimes, late at night, standing out on the terrace, gazing for hours over that huge, dark expanse of moor, the moon hanging over it like some great god's eye, and it was as if he just longed to give himself up to it all. In those moments, I didn't feel like I was in his life at all.

This Park was his world, he patroled and protected it, so I guess it's not surprising he got so upset when the Travellers came. I guess I was pretty upset too. That evening, when he went down again to try to persuade them to move on, I went with him. I thought there'd be more angry words, but he'd changed his tack.

"Look, this is a wild place," he told them. "It's not safe here. You've got women and children—and animals." He nodded at a couple of Dobermans chained up to one of the caravans.

"We're used to wilder places than this, man," Vincent sneered. "You been to the city lately?"

He was a hard-faced guy with a ponytail and a thick silver ring in his nose, which was large and flattish like it had been broken and never mended. A large tattoo of a creature of some kind was emblazoned on one side of his neck.

"Look, don't say I didn't warn you," Dad said, reasonable but tight-lipped. "In the morning I call the authorities in."

I knew that was a bluff. Dad hated "the authorities." I don't believe he'd have called them in even if the Park was swarming with Travellers.

"Hey, don't threaten us, man," said Vincent, pointing at Dad and giving him a tough, small-eyed stare. "We're cool, okay? We're not going to do your little kingdom no harm."

Dad frowned at that, but he didn't say any more. He turned and walked back to the truck and I followed him.

"They don't understand," he muttered gloomily as we drove home. "I'm trying to protect them." He sighed. "I'm trying to protect us all."

That night there was a full moon. A full moon in November out on the moors is some sight. In autumn, when the darkness falls, it really falls, thick and black as treacle, and when the full moon shines, it's something to behold. You can't help but be stirred by it. It's so perfectly round and bright white and, well, lonely somehow. It fills me full of longing and sadness, but I don't know for what. I can understand why it makes wolves howl.

Dad was really edgy that evening. He couldn't settle at all. He was still wandering around when I went to bed. Next morning, when he woke me, he looked like he'd been up all night. After breakfast, he told me to get in the truck, because we were going down to see if those Travellers were still there.

They were. But it didn't look like they were planning on staying much longer. They were packing up to go.

"I see you saw sense," Dad called to Vincent.

The Traveller's leader was humping stuff into the back of a van, where a small child was curled up sleeping. He stopped and turned when Dad spoke and I was taken aback by the change in him. His face was really pale and his eyes looked jumpy.

"I wouldn't stay here any longer if you paid me, man," he said grimly. He bit his lip and frowned. "You'd better come and see this." He led us away from the camp down to the water. Then he gestured at a line of small, scrubby bushes. "In there," he said simply.

210

Dad and I walked past him to the bushes.

Dad jolted and I gasped when I saw what was concealed there. It was the two Dobermans—well, what remained of them. They still had heads and tails but there wasn't an awful lot in between that you could easily identify. Something had torn their bodies apart and devoured bits. What was left was a bloody, gory mess of skin, fur, bone and half-eaten organs. I retched and turned away. Then I threw up by the stream.

After a while, Dad came to find me. I was sitting by the stream with drops of cool water running down my face. He asked me if I was okay and I nodded.

"I warned them," he said gravely, then added, in a tone of relief, "Thank goodness it was only the dogs."

"Yeah," I agreed, thinking of that small child asleep in the back of Vincent's van.

"What do you think could have done it?" I asked.

"I don't know." Dad shrugged. "A big cat maybe. Every moor has its beast, you know. There have been reported sightings of pumas or lynxes on most of the moors in the country at some time or other." But his tone was sceptical.

"You don't think it's a wild cat, do you, Dad?" I pressed.

"It could be." Dad pursed his lips thoughtfully. "Vincent reckons he saw a wolf."

"A wolf!" I exclaimed incredulously, half smiling.

"Yeah," Dad said. "An enormous black wolf with eyes the size of saucers and fangs like butcher's skewers. That's what he said." Dad knew a lot about wolves. As a young man, he'd been part of a wolf-study expedition to Alaska. He loved those animals more than any other—even though he still had a scar on his arm from where one had attacked him.

"It was more likely some stray Rottweiler," I suggested dismissively.

"Perhaps," Dad muttered, still non-committal. "They're going anyway, that's the main thing. We can get on with our lives in peace."

Dad was wrong about that, though. He underestimated the grip that tales of savage beasts roaming the moor can take on people's imagination. Within days of the Travellers' departure, the mauling of the Dobermans had become a local news story and Vincent's giant wolf-creature had been dubbed "The Monster of Monks' Burn." Soon it was picked up by the national news too. The Park was overrun by reporters, who came to our door seeking interviews. Dad was furious.

"Go away!" he shouted, slamming the door on some slavering newshound for about the twentieth time. He wouldn't leave the house because of the reporters, but staying inside drove him mad. After a few days, I'd had enough.

"You've got to talk to them, Dad," I reasoned. "If you don't they'll never go."

But Dad shook his head. "I won't talk to them," he murmured darkly. "They're no better than beasts themselves." He glared at the front door, behind which, we both knew, the cameras and notepads were poised, waiting. "No, they're worse," he growled. "Beasts have a sense of honor."

"Let me talk to them, then," I said calmly. "I'll tell them what they want to know and then they'll go."

Dad couldn't really object to that. So I talked to them. I told them the whole story as I'd seen it. I gave them my opinion that the Monster of Monks' Burn was no more than a savage and hungry stray dog. I'd lived on the moor for twelve years, I said, and there had been no other incident like it. They didn't want to believe that, of course—it wasn't much of a story for them, after all, hardly an exclusive—but eventually they gave up and went away. There's only so much copy you can get out of the death of a couple of dogs, I guess, even when it takes place out on a moor at full-moon.Vincent wasn't exactly the most credible witness either: it turned out that he'd made similarly extravagant claims once before, only then it was about sighting UFOs.

The story of the wolf-creature didn't die, though. We got a lot more visitors than we'd ever had before; many were just ordinary people with a taste for the sensational, but there were the professional snoopers too—weird scientists, so-called investigative journalists, TV researchers. Dad hated them. He considered them to be hostile invaders and did everything he could to drive them off. There was one guy in particular he despised—a really creepy character named Tosh Freeman, who claimed he was writing a book about unnatural creatures. He was the one who started the werewolf rumor.

The creature that Vincent had described could not have been an ordinary wolf, Tosh said. He dismissed too the idea that it might be a big cat that had escaped from a zoo. His theory, if you can call it a theory, was that this was some sort of supernatural beast, a kind of wolf-man or werewolf. Why would anyone take such nonsense seriously, you might ask. Well, I doubt they would have done, if it hadn't been for the fact that the next time there was a full moon, Tosh Freeman had his throat ripped out and his insides opened up and emptied out like a bag of bolognese sauce. Dad found him next morning out on the moor and I was very glad I wasn't with him.

After that, there were police swarming all over the area. The Park was sealed off and a huge hunt began to trap this monstrous, homicidal beast. For days, the police combed the moor, searching for clues, or any sign of the wild animal. But they found nothing: the Monster of Monks' Burn was as elusive as the Loch Ness Monster.

Dad went out each day with the hunt, but only to make sure no major damage was done to his Park and the wildlife that lived there. He cared more for the least of those creatures than for Tosh Freeman or any of the humans, who, he felt, had invaded his home. He was sure the police wouldn't discover anything.

"It'll take more than a bunch of flatfoots to catch this beast," was his contemptuous verdict.

The search seemed to have stirred something in him, though. Even when the police had given up and gone, Dad still paced the moor each day. I didn't know whether it was because he felt there was something out there to uncover or because of his growing restlessness. Certainly, in the days and weeks that followed the unsuccessful monster hunt, Dad was increasingly ill at ease. He couldn't settle at all and when we were together, he hardly spoke a word. When I tried to ask him about it, though, he just shrugged and said it was nothing.

Then one crisp Saturday morning, to my surprise, Dad asked me to go with him in the truck when he drove out over the moor. I needed no second invitation.

We drove for miles with barely a word spoken—Dad deep in his thoughts and I in mine. Finally, in the middle of nowhere, he stopped the truck and nodded to me to get out. I thought maybe we were going to continue on foot, as it was a fine day and both of us loved walking. But Dad stayed by the truck.

"There's something I have to talk to you about, Lucas," he said at last. "You aren't going to like it, but I think it's something you should know. You're old enough now."

"What is it?" I asked, with a mixture of excitement and trepidation. I had no idea what Dad was going to say, but I had a feeling I was finally going to find out what had been eating him these past weeks.

"It's about your mother," Dad went on. "It's about how she died." He looked at me with eyes so naked with pain that my throat tightened. I'd always been told my mother died in an accident. "Your mother killed herself," Dad muttered.

"She killed herself!" I gasped. "But why?" I hadn't expected anything like this. I was shaking my head and my breathing had become a bewildered pant.

"She was very unhappy," Dad answered, and he gave me a piercing look. "There are some things, some horrors, that cannot be borne," he said quietly. "The only way to escape is to die. I think you're old enough now to know that."

"No," I howled, my throat so tight I could hardly breathe. "No, I don't know that! I won't believe that!" I turned and kicked the truck. Then I began beating the metal with my fists.

"Lucas! Lucas!" Dad called and his big hands locked like

handcuffs around my wrists. Then I just sort of fell against him and he hugged me like he hadn't done for years and years, and I started to cry like maybe I'd never cried before. All these years I'd been robbed of a mom—and she was the one who'd robbed me. Having a child was supposed to make you happy, wasn't it? How could she have killed herself when she had me to love and look after?

The days that followed were hell for me. Dad was kind and attentive, but there was nothing he could say to reassure me. The truth was plain to see and it made me feel like those Dobermans or Tosh Freeman, with my guts all churned up and savaged. It seemed to me like Mom had committed suicide to get away from me. She hadn't loved me enough to want to stay. So what was wrong with me? Was I some kind of monster? Dad told me over and over that it wasn't because of me she had killed herself. It was despite me, despite her love for me. The darkness, the pain, had been too much for her.

"What darkness? What pain?" I demanded.

But Dad didn't answer. He just looked at me with his extraordinary, intense eyes that were like wounds. "It should have been me," was all he said. "I'm the one who should have died." But when I asked him what he meant, he wouldn't explain, which only made things worse.

I was still feeling pretty raw the night Dad came into my room and told me to put on my coat and boots, because we were going out. I glanced toward the window and saw a full moon staring in. Then I saw the rifle in Dad's hand.

"It's time to put an end to all this," Dad said grimly. "The beast must be destroyed."

That made me sit up, because I hadn't thought that Dad really believed there was a beast out there. I mean, even after Tosh Freeman's death, I thought he shared my opinion that it was some sort of savage stray dog that was responsible.

"Do you really think there's a beast out here?" I asked as we walked out on to the moor.

Dad sighed. "There's a beast out here, sure enough," he said, kind of sadly. He looked up at the moon. "And tonight it's got to be killed." The idea of killing any wild thing was abhorrent to Dad, I knew that—especially one that had taken refuge in his Park.

"But why, Dad?" I asked. "And why tonight?"

"Because tonight there's a full moon and that's when this beast attacks," he replied. "While it lives, no one is safe. If it's not destroyed, then one night it might be you who's its victim."

"Me!" The suggestion seemed ludicrous somehow. Anyway it was Dad who walked out on the moors at night, not me. "More likely you," I said.

"I don't care about myself," Dad shrugged. "But I won't put your life at risk. Heaven knows, I've done enough damage already." He pursed his lips doggedly. "It's my responsibility to put an end to all this."

I guessed he meant that it was his duty as the Warden of the Park, so I didn't question him any further and we walked on in silence.

The moon was playing weird games that night. It vacillated back and forth through the wispy veil of cloud that drifted continuously across the sky. When the moon came forward, it shone so fiercely that it was too bright to look at; then it fell back and back, vanishing into the dense gloom, until it was the merest outline. And then nothing. No moon. A chilling, all-consuming darkness. Moments passed, the clouds rushed by, and then the moon appeared again, rampaging forward, perfectly round and dazzling. I'd never seen anything like it.

It was in such a moment of glaring brilliance that Dad stopped walking. He looked up with unwavering eyes.

"The time has come," he said. He passed me the rifle. "Take this." He stood quite still, as if listening for something. I felt the tension in him. As the moon started to fall away and the light faded, I began to shiver. There was ice on my spine and it felt like every hair on my head and body was being tweaked mercilessly. Back and back the moon shuffled, vanishing into darkness, until it was gone entirely.

And then I knew the beast had come.

I could sense it there close by in the blackness. I couldn't see it, but I could hear its whispery, phantomlike breathing. It was there alright and I was scared stiff. I moved closer to where I thought Dad must be, the rifle gripped tightly in my clammy hands. I wished it was Dad who had the gun. I could use it—I'd practiced many times—but right now I was too petrified even to squeeze a trigger.

The moon rose again, hurrying forward, bringing light, illuminating the creature before me. I caught my breath, swallowed. Sweat trickled from my armpit down my side as I took in what I was seeing. It was a wolf. But not an ordinary wolf. This was the monster wolf that Vincent had described. It was black and enormous, with huge, fanglike teeth. It was the eyes, though, that held me. They were not a beast's eyes, they were human and they were not fierce, but pleading.

And then at last I understood.

The eyes looked from my face to the rifle in my hands, then back again, beseeching, imploring. But I shook my head and my body shuddered with horror. I would not do it. Could not do it. Still the eyes begged me. But they were changing now—yellowing, hardening, dehumanizing. In moments the metamorphosis was complete. Now I was face to face with a monstrous, murderous beast; a beast that I knew would destroy me. There was nothing of Dad left.

Seeing this decided me. When the beast leaped, I fired, without hesitation, once, twice, three times. The bullets, as I discovered later, had been made by Dad himself out of silver. And they didn't fail him. The werewolf was dead. It lay at my feet, still and beautiful, all its terrible savagery gone. But it was not the beast I wept for as I fell to my knees beside it in the moonlight. It was for Dad, it was for me, it was for Mom.

The note Dad left explained what he could not tell me to my face. How, having been bitten by an unusually vicious wolf in Alaska, he had found himself frighteningly transformed by the full moon. How, when Mom found out, it had affected her mind so badly that she had killed herself. How Dad had tried to stay away from people until I was old enough for him to leave me. But that had become impossible.

He made arrangements for me, of course—my education and everything was all taken care of. I am provided for—that's what Dad's lawyer says. Provided for. How empty those words sound. It's Dad's words in that final note that ring in my ears, over and over, his voice pleading for understanding.

Well, I do understand, Dad. Now I understand everything. But that does not stop me walking out over the moor some nights—nights like tonight, when the moon is full and bright —and howling,

howling,

howling.

# ACKNOWLEDGMENTS

The publisher would like to thank the copyright holders for permission to reproduce the following copyright material:

**Woody Allen:** "Count Dracula" from *Getting Even* by Woody Allen. Copyright © 1971 by Woody Allen. Reprinted by permission of Random House, Inc. **Angela Carter:** "The Werewolf" from *The Bloody Chamber and Other Stories* by Angela Carter. Copyright © Angela Carter 1979. Reproduced by permission of the Estate of Angela Carter c/o Rogers, Coleridge & White Ltd., 20 Powis Mews, London W11 1JN. **August Derleth:** "The Drifting Snow" copyright © 1948 by August Derleth. Reprinted by permission of Arkham House Publishers, Inc. **Arthur Conan Doyle:** "The Adventure of the Sussex Vampire" copyright © 1996 The Sir Arthur Conan Doyle Copyright Holders. Reprinted by kind permission of Jonathan Clowes Ltd., London, on behalf of Andrea Plunket, Administrator of the Sir Arthur Conan Doyle Copyrights. **Winifred Finlay:** "Terror in the Tatras" from *Vampires, Werewolves, and Phantoms of the Night* by Winifred Finlay (Methuen Children's Books Ltd. 1983.) Copyright © 1983 Winifred Finlay. Reprinted by permission of Reed Consumer Books Ltd. **Carl Jacobi:** "Revelations in Black" copyright © 1933 by Carl Jacobi. Reprinted by permission of Arkham House Publishers, Inc. **Anthony Masters:** "Freeze-Up" from *Werewolf Stories to Tell in the Dark* by Anthony Masters (Puffin Books 1996.) Copyright © Anthony Masters 1996. Reprinted by permission of The Peters Fraser and Dunlop Group Ltd., on behalf of the author. **Richard Matheson:** "Drink My Blood" from *Imagination* (as "Blood Son") by Richard Matheson. Copyright © 1951, renewed 1979 by Richard Matheson. Reprinted by permission of Don Congdon Associates, Inc. **William F. Nolan:** "Getting Dead" copyright

# ACKNOWLEDGMENTS

© 1991 by William F. Nolan. Reprinted by permission of the author. **Barbara Leonie Picard:** "The Werewolf" from *French Legends, Tales, and Fairy Stories* retold by Barbara Leonie Picard (OUP 1955.) Copyright © Barbara Leonie Picard 1955. Reprinted by permission of the author. **Jane Yolen:** "Mama Gone" by Jane Yolen. Copyright © 1991 by Jane Yolen. First appeared in *Vampires: A Collection of Orginal Stories*, edited by Jane Yolen and Martin H. Greenberg, published by HarperCollins Publishers. Reprinted by permission of Curtis Brown, Ltd. **Roger Zelazny:** "Dayblood" copyright © 1985 The Amber Corporation. Permission granted by The Pimlico Agency, Inc., agents for the estate of Roger Zelazny.

Every effort has been made to obtain permission to reproduce copyright material but there may be cases where we have been unable to contact a copyright holder. The publisher will be happy to correct any omissions in future printings.

# Titles in the Story Library Series